JAMAICAN TRANSIT

by
Judy Goodrobb

ISBN: 9798515856472

Cover photo: Robert Adler

To Robert, who gave me my first typewriter and told me I was a writer. To Natalie, who inspired me. To Liz and Erin, who taught me so much. And to Jane and PJ, who helped me through so many drafts.

This is a time of endings and beginnings. If you have built your life up to now around activities inappropriate for you, it will be a period of crisis.

Robert Hand, *Planets in Transit*

CHAPTER ONE

Fourth of July. Independence Day.

Joanna sat on the porch between the two men. She watched the dark sea churn. The rain fell in gray sheets, torrents pounding with a deafening drum on the flimsy, tin roof. Hardly a glimmer of light escaped through the flag shrouding the window behind them.

She laughed softly, just loud enough for Michael to hear. He sat close by. She could feel the warmth from his body although they weren't touching. After nine years together, she imagined he probably sensed her chuckle as much as heard it.

"What's so funny?" he asked.

In the strobe of a lightning bolt, Joanna saw a half smile on his face, more a smirk really, or maybe a question, as if he weren't sure whether or not he should be laughing, too. She heard the staccato rap of his foot on the concrete floor of the porch. She could barely make out the piston-like motion of his knee in the fading flash, but she sensed it, and knew it meant he was uptight about something.

"Hmm, nothing really. It's just weird that we're in Jamaica watching lightening instead of home watching fireworks on the Fourth of July." She fingered the beads on her necklace.

To her right, their friend Dave snorted. "A whole lot better than that patriotic bullshit back home." Dressed in tank top and cut-off jeans, Dave tilted back in his chair and gazed out at the storm. He oozed a sleepy sensuality, totally laid-back, totally cool.

A crack of thunder boomed. Joanna jumped, sure the ground

shook.

She tried to think of home. They had only been in Jamaica a few days, but even so, she could barely remember home. The lazy rhythms of the island stretched out the minutes and hours. Every day felt like a month. Still the languid cadences of the island had done little to relax either her or Michael. The tension between them was like the storm, crackling with a charge that could explode at any time.

A voice floated from the shadows behind Joanna where Jeevan lounged against the stuccoed wall. "Hey, mahn, smoke some *h*erb?"

Jeevan leaned forward, and Joanna saw a flash reflected in his mirror sunglasses. She could just make out the stars and stripes, white and orange, of the knit cap he wore as the light subsided. He had come to bring them ganja, "*h*erb" as he called it, pronouncing the "h." He had joined them on the porch when the downpour started. His hat seemed to glow in the eerie storm-light above his shadowed face.

"Jeevan, did you wear that hat for the Fourth of July?" Michael asked.

Jeevan swept the hat from his head, turning it over and inspecting it as if he had forgotten what it looked like. "Dis? No, mahn, dis my *hat*, mahn. Dis me number one hat." Jeevan leaned forward and nudged Dave playfully on the shoulder. "Smoke some *h*erb, mahn?"

Dave reached into his shirt pocket and handed a thin joint to Jeevan, who laughed as he snatched it.

"Hey, dis plenty for me, mahn. Whad *yuh* gonna smoke?"

A reggae song floated through the window from the bar behind them, and Joanna's senses seemed to slow in time with the music, the unhurried heartbeat of the island. The music swept over her like a wave, submerging her in a seductive, hazy warmth along with the heat and humidity that dripped in the air.

They had hired a taxi at the airport in Montego Bay and endured a crazy, whirlwind drive to Negril, a small fishing village where they were staying at High Hat's for a month. They needed the time together if they were going to pull their relationship back from the brink.

But that very first afternoon, they had met Dave and had fallen into an instant friendship, the way people do on vacations when time is slow, and the only demands are food, sun, and sleep. From the moment she saw Dave, Joanna felt a connection to him; he reminded her of someone, maybe some actor, a friend, a long-lost cousin. She didn't know.

"It's really cool you're from Philly, too," Dave said. "I miss the old homestead sometimes." He reeled off a list of names they might know. None clicked.

"I know I know you from somewhere, Dave," Joanna said.

She turned to Michael. "Doesn't he remind you of someone?"

"Not really."

Another crack of thunder sounded.

"Hey, mahn, Ah not jokin'. Yuh must light some more *herb* for yuhself and yuh friends," Jeevan said.

Joanna watched the orange glow of the joint as Jeevan inhaled. It flickered and cast a fleeting glimmer on his face with each toke, and the stripes on his cap seemed to dance in rhythm with the hissing of his breath as he dragged on the joint.

Dave whipped another from his pocket, lit it, and handed it to Joanna. She hesitated.

"Is it cool to smoke out in the open?" she asked.

"Sure, mahn. Is cool, mahn," Jeevan said, drawling his words through lips frozen in the short glare of the lightning. "Babylon long gone."

Michael started. "What the…?"

"Is cool, mahn. Babylon de police. Dey far, far away, now."

The rain had begun to slacken, but flashes of lightning stabbed through the dark sky over the lapping sea. Joanna counted to herself: one, two, three, four. The crash of thunder rumbled all around them as the storm moved out over the roiling water.

"It's moving out to sea," she said over the last murmur of the peal. She waited for the sound to stop and passed Michael the stub of the joint. "Anyone up for a beer inside?" she asked. "I've had enough fireworks."

The men murmured their agreement and rose to go to the bar. As she slid between the chairs, making her way to the open entrance, she felt firm hands encircle the back of her waist, as if to guide her. She hesitated, and then the hands were gone. In the darkness, she couldn't be sure whose hands had touched her.

CHAPTER TWO

This was not the first trip to Jamaica for Joanna and Michael. They had vacationed here several times, always for a week or so. But this time was different. They planned to stay a month, maybe even longer. They were free to spend the time because the dog was dead. It was strange. They had named her Reggae because they loved the island, its mystery, its hypnotic rhythms, its ganja. But now she was dead, killed in a gruesome accident with a train, and they were here, enjoying the sun, the fun, and the weed. Sometimes Joanna felt as if, in a weird way, the dog had given them this gift, a chance to start their relationship again, a month to heal themselves. If they could.

But now, the hot sun burned these thoughts from Joanna's mind. The sweltering sphere beat down mercilessly filling the air with a brightness that hurt her eyes. Hot waves rose from the deserted dirt road in front of her, the air swollen with heat and humidity. She sat with Michael in the shade of High Hat's porch, her visor pulled down low on the bridge of her nose while he hid behind his mirrored shades. It was one in the afternoon and too oppressive to be anywhere but in the shade or in the ocean. They sipped on lukewarm Red Stripes, slowly moving the bottles to their mouths as if fighting some invisible current. The beers were only meant to cool them; they were already high on Jeevan's ganja.

On the other side of the road, a narrow ribbon of beach skirted the ocean. A gnarled sea grape tree heavy with round green fruit framed the two small sailboats that lay on their sides in the sand as if exhausted by the heat. Joanna was tempted to lie down herself on the floor of the porch but couldn't seem to find the energy to move. The ganja and the whisper of the sea were doing their work, and Joanna felt as mellow as a cat napping on a sunny windowsill. Maybe Jamaica would be the charm, and she and Michael could find their groove again.

Michael leaned down to pick up a newspaper. Joanna watched the jerky motion of his body as he reached forward. His arms and shoulders were well-formed, and his slim legs and hips gave him the lank look of a swimmer. Still, Joanna sighed, thinking how long it had been since she felt a really strong desire for Michael. Too long, way too long. Of course, she still wanted him, but not so much for sex as out of some deep need to be connected to him, to feel the security of his arms around her.

Michael raised the paper to eye level, struggling against the same currents that weighed down the beer bottles. He waved the paper in front of him, trying to fold it in half, and fanned himself. The motion sent ripples towards Joanna of warm, murky air, which did little to cool her. She pushed her hand through the humid air and set her Red Stripe on the railing of the porch.

"You might as well forget the fanning," she said, but somehow the words came out garbled, and she saw a lazy stream of word bubbles floating from her mouth. "All that moving ... only makes you ... hotter," she said. She swatted at the bubbles, but they escaped her grasp.

Michael swiveled his head to face her and smiled. "It's something to do." He raised his free hand slowly towards her, and Joanna wondered if he saw the bubbles that floated in front of her face. Instead, he waved his hand in the air close to her nose. "A bug," he said with a Cheshire cat grin. "This is great stuff, isn't it? Wonder what's in it?"

Joanna stared at him wild-eyed. "What do you mean?" The word bubbles burst, pierced by her voice.

Michael slowly maneuvered his head like some electric mannequin in a store window and looked up at her. He opened his mouth to speak, and Joanna imagined she could hear the words forming before he uttered them. She waited, sure his voice would sound like a 45 RPM record played at 33.

"Calm ... down ... and ... enjoy... yourself," he drawled. "Don't get freaked out. I was kidding. There's nothing in the weed. Just good Jamaican ganja."

Joanna shot up and paced the length of the porch. The sweat ran down her face, her neck, between her breasts. She felt the stickiness under her arms, in the creases behind her knees and at her elbows. She felt her nose flatten into her cheeks, her mouth stretch into a downward clown curve, her arms and legs turn to rubber. She was a puddle of flesh, bright swirls of blue and purple, the remnants of her steaming shorts and top, circling within it.

"Sit down and relax. Weed used to make you really mellow," Michael said, reaching to pull her down into the chair. "How can you relax if you keep pacing?"

She yanked her arm out of his grasp and glared at him.

"Jo, you've got to stop being so uptight. We're supposed to be having a good time, right?" He was smiling, but his watery eyes seemed to look right through Joanna as if he were concentrating on something beyond her.

She clutched the railing. Did the floor just move? She glanced over her shoulder toward the ocean, her thoughts tumbling inside her head. He clearly didn't care anymore, not like when they were first together. He used to reassure her, try to talk her out of it when she got nervous about something. Just the sound of his voice, his touch, was enough to make her fears subside. But now, he seemed impatient with her anxieties, especially after Reggae got killed. She shuddered.

Even here in the hot sun of the Jamaican afternoon, she could still imagine the dog's severed blond head on the tracks. Now, the dull hiss of the ocean took on an ominous tone. She turned to Michael.

"Michael, I'm anxious."

"I know. You're always anxious." He kept his eyes on the newspaper.

"I am not always nervous. It's what you said about the weed. And also, about Reggae. Maybe we shouldn't have come to Jamaica."

"Jo, the reason we're staying for a month is because the dog's dead." Michael's face seemed to wobble like a rubber Halloween mask.

"That's what I mean. It's like we're having more fun because she's dead."

"Jo, don't be ridiculous."

Joanna turned to look toward the sea. "I'll feel better if we take a walk."

"Okay, go take a walk." His eyes were glued to the paper.

Joanna stared at him, her mouth set in a tight, thin line. "Together. I mean, let's take a walk together."

He smacked the paper onto his lap and glared at her. "Jo, I don't want to take a walk. If you think a walk will make you feel better, then take a walk. You don't need me."

She glowered at him. "I thought we were supposed to spend time together. Isn't that why we're here?"

He lifted the paper again but dropped it almost immediately. He jumped up and slammed his beer on the railing next to Joanna. She got up, thinking he had changed his mind and wanted to walk with her. But instead, he leaned over the porch. She heard a noise off in the distance, a hubbub like a mob of people.

"What is that?" she asked, gripping the railing. She imagined hordes of people running at them.

"I don't know."

Michael craned his head around the side of the porch. The commotion grew closer, louder, until it was just around the bend in the road. Joanna could hear voices shouting out in patois. Michael bounded over the railing, knocking the Red Stripe off, and landed with a thud in the sand. He sprang up and moved toward the voices.

"Michael, come back."

He dismissed Joanna with a back-handed wave. A small shack sailed around the bend, surrounded by a crowd of men. Some ran; some walked; others hung out the windows and doors like firemen on a hook and ladder. The cottage seemed to float four feet off the ground, its base hidden by the men pushing it. The noise ratcheted up as the men laughed and shouted at each other, passing spliffs from hand to hand.

Michael turned to Joanna, eyes ablaze like a madman's. "I can't believe it. They're moving a whole house by hand!" He waded toward the moving shack, carefully placing one foot in front of the other, as if sloshing through water.

Joanna followed him down the steps. He was so stoned. He was going to do something crazy. Several men motioned to him, their grins wild, big gaping holes where their teeth were missing. Michael ran towards the shack. Joanna covered her face as he leaped but looked just in time to see him fly, arms outstretched toward the Jamaicans who hoisted him up. Holding onto a window jamb, he seemed to float in the wind of the sailing house. He let out a howl.

Joanna clenched her fists. "No!"

A Rasta, black locks streaming from his head, jumped from the house and sauntered toward her with slow, undulating movements, as if dancing to some unhurried music in his head. He stuck his face close to Joanna's and whispered, his eyes red and heavy-lidded, "Is okay, mahn. Yuh mahn come bahk someday." He opened his mouth wide, and a blast of laughter and smoke, reeking of weed, poured over Joanna. She rushed past the Rasta.

"Michael! Come back, you bastard!"

He never even acknowledged her, and she watched as the house disappeared around the next bend in the road with Michael hanging on. She stood fuming at the empty space, jaw tight, too stunned to move. When the voices had finally faded, she raised her fist and shook it at the deserted road, then turned and started back toward the porch, kicking sand as she did.

What had happened to the Michael Joanna fell in love with? That Michael would never leave her stranded on the side of a Jamaican road. But that night when Reggae was killed, things had seemed to change. She had expected him to comfort her as always, but instead he had insisted on going back to his studio to work. Distraught, she had pleaded with him. "Michael. How can you leave me? I can't be alone tonight." But her need hadn't swayed him. Finally, he had begrudgingly agreed to her going with him to the studio.

She shook her head, sending the memory fleeing. She climbed the stairs into the shade of High Hat's porch. If Michael was going to act like an idiot, she wasn't about to just stand there and act stupid herself. She plopped into a chair and grabbed the one Red Stripe still on the railing, then snatched the paper at her feet. She tried to read but the words danced in front of her eyes. She hurled the paper down and smacked the beer onto the railing. "Screw you!" she said aloud and stood, jamming her hand into her shorts pocket. The key to the room! Where was the key? She shoved her hand into the other pocket. Nothing. She plucked her day pack from behind the chair and began rifling through it, pulling things out, tossing them above her head like a crazed magician pulling scarves from a hat until its contents were strewn at her feet. She turned the pack upside down, then flung it on top of the pile in disgust.

"Shit! No key. He took the fucking key." She slumped down into the chair and stared out toward the beach where a young boy sat in the crook of the sea grape tree, watching her. His bare legs stuck out from a ragged pair of shorts and dangled in the air below him. A faint smile played across his face. Joanna reddened and stooped to shovel the pile back into her pack. Then slinging it over her shoulder, she turned and walked toward the side of the building where a door opened into the little bar. She hesitated at the doorway, then reached into her pocket, pulled out some money and counted it. "Hell with him," she muttered and strode up to the bar.

High Hat lolled alone behind the counter, arranging glasses on the shelves along a back wall. He swiveled in slow motion to face her and smiled.

"A beer, please," she said, sliding onto a stool.

"Where yuh mahn?" he asked, placing a Red Stripe on the counter.

"I don't really know," she said, "and I don't really care." She took off her visor and slapped it onto the stool next to her.

High Hat stopped wiping and shook his head.

"He went running after that shack that went by. Did you see it?" Joanna said, sipping on her beer. "Can you give me another key if he doesn't come back?"

High Hat laughed. "Oh, mahn, 'im come bahk. 'Im havin' some fun, dat's all. Yuh t'ink 'im leave a pretty t'ing like you?"

High Hat looked to be around fifty with the sinewy shoulders and arms of a construction worker. Joanna watched the bulge of his biceps as he wiped around her beer with a cloth and imagined him hauling in fishing nets heavy with a good catch from the sea.

She smiled and swung around on the bar stool to gaze out the windows that lined the small barroom. The branches of a squat palm tree reached through the screen-less frames into the bar, stirring a bit in the breeze, inside and out, so that the tree seemed a part of the room. A tiny hut with intense sky-blue shutters faced the bar, and a blond-coated dog, tied close to the hut, strained at the lead. Joanna choked on her beer. It looked like Reggae. But, no, it was just another blond dog. She had to stop thinking about the dog.

The young boy had left his spot in the sea grape tree and ambled along the dirt road, which wound past the barroom and up the hill. Joanna watched his slow movements, feeling her body relax. The beer was cooling her; it made her legs tingle, loosening the tightness in them as if the liquid flowed through her veins. High Hat returned to wiping glasses at the sink near the end of the bar, and she realized that, of course, he was right. Michael would come back. Still, how could he leave her stranded? A Rolling Stones' song floated through her mind: "Carry the lantern high ..."

"Hear that?" Michael used to say when she was uptight. "I'll do that for you; I'll carry the lantern high. I'll go first, so there'll always be light, and you won't have to be afraid."

But those days seemed a long time ago, now. It was stupid, really, but she had taken him seriously, had believed him, then, when they were first together. She had felt so secure, knowing he would protect her. But now, sitting here alone at this bar in Jamaica, she felt betrayed and afraid, as if something dark and immense were gaining on her, something she had been running from for a long time.

High Hat's sing-song lilt floated over her, "Anudder Red Stripe, mahn?"

Joanna swung around and shrugged, "Sure, why not?" She watched him reach down into the cooler when she felt an arm slide around her shoulders. "Michael," she said, turning to face him.

"Sorry. It's only me," Dave said.

He dropped his arm and slipped onto the stool next to her, grinning like a man with a secret he wasn't telling. She smiled back. His cut-off jeans showed off his long, lean legs, tanned to a sugary brown by months in the Jamaican sun. His brown hair had receded some, leaving just a few wispy curls on his high forehead. Joanna fought an urge to twirl those strands around her finger and laughed. The scent that wafted from him seemed familiar, a faint, musky smell laced with a hint of coconut oil. She inhaled a deep breath of his beach scent. They sat in comfortable silence as if they had often met like this before.

"Hey. What are you doing here? No touristas to take sailing?" she asked.

"I took a few out today and just dropped off two who were staying here. Saw you sitting all alone and decided to keep you company." He motioned toward High Hat. "Uno Red Stripe, por favor, mahn," he said.

High Hat bent over the cooler as they both watched silently. He popped the top off and placed the beer in front of Dave, who gulped down half the bottle.

"I was thirsty," he said, swallowing hard. "Where's your old man?"

"I don't know where the hell he is."

Dave whistled. "Really, mahn?" They sat sipping their beers while High Hat wiped the counter. "Thanks, mahn. We're cool," Dave said.

High Hat frowned and walked toward the door to the kitchen. When he was gone, Dave said, "You guys have a fight or something?"

"Yeah, or something." Joanna ran her finger up the side of the beer bottle, intent on drawing a line through the beads of water condensed there. She wondered how much she should tell Dave. Maybe he would think she was a bitch. She turned to look at him; he smiled and nodded. "No, not a fight, really" she said. "Actually, he just ran off after a bunch of crazy Jamaicans who were hauling a shack down the road. Left me here without a key, so I can't even get into the room to piss." She flicked a book of matches lying on the counter onto the floor. "And didn't even bother to say good-bye. That's all."

"You're mad, huh?"

"Moi?" Joanna raised her eyebrows in mock disbelief.

Dave took another sip from his beer while Joanna sank back into connecting the drops on her beer bottle. She shifted on her stool, swung around to look behind her, then leaned in close. "Got any weed?" she asked.

"Sure. Back at my cabin. Wanna get high?"

Joanna hesitated. Michael wouldn't know where she was. Maybe he would worry. Screw him, she thought. Why should she care? Smiling, she jumped from the stool. "Definitely. Let's do it."

Dave reached into his back pocket and pulled out some bills. "What did you have?"

"Two Red Stripes."

He threw a couple of bills on the counter and swiveled off his stool. "Okay. Let's go," he said, taking Joanna by the elbow and steering her toward the door. "I have to go tie up my boat first. Come on."

On the road, the sun beat down, a hot blast from a huge oven, but the beers helped to make the temperature bearable. Joanna felt comfortably fluid as she walked next to Dave toward the beach where his sailboat lay on its side in the sand.

"Sit here while I tie it up," he said.

A slight breeze blew over her as the waves hissed against the beach. Joanna sat down and stuck her hand in the hot sand, grabbing a handful and letting the gritty grains run through her fingers. She shaded her eyes and watched Dave as he worked on the boat. He moved from one side of the boat to the other, tying the sail with thick ropes to hooks located on either side and then did the same with the mast. His motions were familiar although she didn't know the slightest thing about boats. Yet, she seemed to know what he would do next, almost before he did it, as if she remembered sitting here, under the blazing sun watching him. But it couldn't be. She had never been here before with him. She swallowed. What was going on? Was it the ganja? A hot current rushed from her head, down her torso, into her legs, and vanished like water into the grains below her, leaving her empty. She wrapped her arms around her shoulders trying to calm herself.

A sudden movement caught her attention. Dave had stopped working and was reaching up to pull his t-shirt off. He walked over, shirt in hand, his back to the sun. His face was a black hole against the corona of the sun. She couldn't make out his features, and, for a sickening moment, she couldn't remember what he looked like.

"Hold this for me, will you?" he said, turning slightly, bringing his features back into focus. He tossed his shirt to her, and she caught it, her reflex motion breaking the spell. Relax, she told herself and smiled at him. Dave moved back to the boat, stopped, and looked over his shoulder at her. "You know, it's weird," he said. "It's like we've been here before. Déjà vu, right?"

Joanna stared at him, wide-eyed. Shit! He was reading her mind. She swallowed hard. Sand seemed to line her throat. She struggled to speak but managed to croak out. "I sort of felt it, too."

Dave didn't answer but stood motionless. An unnatural stillness seemed to fall over the beach. She couldn't hear the ocean. She couldn't speak. She couldn't move. Why didn't he answer? Why had everything stopped? The taste of stale beer welled in her throat. "Dave? Can we go now?" Her voice seemed to come from a small metal box in her throat. It vibrated, setting off a tremor of fear through her insides. She jumped up.

"What's the matter?" Dave reached for her.

She stood still, his hand on her arm, then leaned backwards and carefully dusted the sand from the back of her legs. "Nothing," she said. "Nothing. It just made me a little nervous that you're feeling it, too, you know, that we've been here before. I mean, I was just having the same feeling. Do you think it means something?" She laughed uneasily.

"Yeah, it means we're both high," he said and chuckled. "I'll be done soon. I just have to get the boat away from the water." He walked around to the front of the boat and began hauling it further up the beach, away from the rising tide. Joanna walked toward him.

"Here, let me help," she said, relieved to have something to do. Tucking his shirt into her waistband, she leaned over, and together they dragged the boat to a point nearer the road.

"That should keep it," he said, tying it to a post. "That was a lot easier with the two of us. Thanks."

Joanna smiled and pulled his shirt from her waist and handed it to him.

He slid it over his head. "Mmmm, smells good. Like you," he said and grinned.

CHAPTER THREE

They hopped over the low stone wall at the edge of the beach and walked along the road toward the compound where Dave rented a small cottage from Momma Samuel. As they reached the top of the steep hill that led to the cottage, Joanna could see the old woman squatting by a fire in the yard, surrounded by at least a dozen children. A large, black pot hung from a sturdy tripod above the fire. Momma Samuel crouched, slicing yams for the evening meal into a simmering stew. She was slight, but her thin arms were roped with muscles.

Dave leaned in close to Joanna's ear, "She's amazing. She does everything around here. Treats me really well. Cleans, cooks, does my wash. Can you imagine your grandmother doing all that?"

Momma Samuel looked up and saw the two Americans approaching. She passed the yam she held to a young girl, stood, and wiped her hands on her apron.

"Hello, Momma Samuel," Dave said.

"Hello, hello. Good day, good day, yes, a very good day." She spoke rapidly, continuing to wipe her hands.

"Momma Samuel, this is my friend Joanna."

Joanna nodded and smiled as the old woman neared them.

"Oh, very nice to meet yuh, missy," Momma Samuel said, bobbing her head in a kind of bow. She tilted her head and stared at Joanna. "Yuh come stay with us."

It wasn't really a question, and something about the woman's tone seemed to Joanna as if she been expecting her. Joanna wrote it off as simply Momma Samuel's warm welcome. Joanna laughed and looked at Dave, who seemed to be waiting for her answer, too. "No, thank you, Momma Samuel. I'm just visiting. But your home looks like a lovely place to stay. Maybe next time I'm in Jamaica."

"Oh," Momma Samuel took Joanna's hand. Her kind eyes crinkled and took on a warm glow. She locked eyes with Joanna. "Maybe soon come."

Joanna cocked her head with a sideways smile, puzzled by the woman's intensity.

Dave motioned to Joanna and moved toward the cottage. "I'll see you for supper, Momma Samuel," he said, over his shoulder.

"Oh, yes, yes, supper," the old woman smiled and glided back to the children.

Dave and Joanna walked onto the small porch where three wicker chairs huddled together. Half of the building was built of cinder blocks painted the color of coral while the other half, clearly tacked on, was covered with wood siding. Screens and louvered glass covered the windows in the new section. By the look of the house, Joanna guessed Momma Samuel was very well off by Negril standards. The other buildings in the compound and the other homes Joanna had seen so far were simply shacks, stuck together from odd bits of lumber, with roofs of rusted corrugated steel, plastic, or tar paper and screenless windows open to the air.

"This is Momma Samuel's house," Dave said. "She rents it to tourists for the extra money. I've been here about six months." He motioned to a ramshackle house across the narrow dirt road. "She stays over there with her daughter when it's rented."

They climbed the few steps to the porch where he took Joanna's arm and guided her toward the front door, holding the screen door open. "Let's get high first. Then we can sit on the porch." Joanna stepped into a cool, dark room as familiar to her as a memory from a recurring dream. She hesitated, realizing she had never been here before. How could she remember it?

"Momma Samuel calls this the 'parlor,'" Dave said, sweeping his hand through the air to indicate the room and ending with a low bow to Joanna.

The space was bare except for two wooden folding chairs, a small coffee table, and a framed crucifix on the wall. A vase full of fake yellow flowers sat on the table. Dave led Joanna to a room with a low chest of drawers and a metal frame bed. "My bedroom," he said, bowing low again.

Clothing was strewn in heaps among mounds of books. A full-length mirror leaned against the wall with a suitcase propped at its base to hold it upright. A sign over the bed read, "Just Passing Through."

Joanna pointed at the sign and laughed. "Appropriate."

"Yeah, I haven't really settled in yet, I guess." He gave Joanna a slow smile. "Sort of how my whole life's been so far." He pointed to a beaded curtain that hung across the doorway to the next room. "This is the kitchen, obviously," he said, holding the beads back for Joanna to pass through.

She stepped into a narrow, bright room. A sink and a little counter on rickety legs lined the wall to the right of the door. Over the sink, a small window opened onto a view of a green yard. The center of the room was overtaken with a Formica table and two tattered kitchen chairs, the stuffing bursting through holes in their vinyl cushions. The kitchen felt comfortable to Joanna. She imagined it was a room where she could spend a lot of time, gazing out the window to the lush, dense backyard. She moved toward the back door that looked out onto a wooden stall a short distance from the cottage. "What's that?" she asked, pointing.

"The shower," Dave said, coming to stand behind her, close enough so that she could feel her hair stir as he breathed. She inhaled his scent, that mix of coconut oil and something heavier, gamier, a trace of a men's locker room. The heat from their bodies seemed to mingle in the space between them, connecting them, and she felt a tingling along her back as if his shadow were touching her there. From somewhere in the compound, Joanna heard a slap, slap, slap—the cadence mixing with the ebb and flow of children's laughter and the faint hum of women's conversation floating on the air. Someone, probably Momma Samuel, was pounding yams for the family's meal. For a moment, Joanna and Dave seemed to sway back and forth to the rhythm, moving together as if wrapped in a single fabric. But then a dog howled in the distance, and the fabric fell away.

Dave spoke first. "Let's get high," he said, stepping back.

Joanna wavered slightly, like a reed released by his passing. She reached out for the doorframe to steady herself. "I'll be right there," she said. "I just want to check out the backyard a bit."

He watched her for a moment, shrugged, then walked out of the kitchen.

Joanna stepped down to amble past the shower to the brush that ringed the backyard. The growth was wild with tough grasses and shrubs, tinted a silvery gray-green, the color of marijuana plants. It was as if the sandy soil gave up just enough moisture to produce, not a true green, but only a hint of color. A sea-grape tree reached toward the cottage with twisted limbs, its roots spreading into the sand of the yard. Small clumps of vegetation grew scattered along the border of the enclosure as if only the daily tread of bare feet kept the growth from encroaching too far, kept the jungle and its wildness at bay.

Sumac-like shrubs with long slender branches and evenly-spaced rows of narrow leaves looked just like the trees that had grown in the deserted lot behind her house when she was a child. Strange, she thought, that trees so similar would grow in climates so different. Here, of course, they grew taller and fuller, but she remembered playing "jungle" among the city weeds with her neighbor Jay, hacking through the sumacs with their imaginary axes. Joanna frowned, stepped back, then stared at the trees. That was it. It was Jay. Dave reminded her of Jay. She hadn't thought of Jay for years although she had had one intense crush on him long ago. But what a weird coincidence—the sumac trees, Dave, Jay. She spun around, frowning again, and hurried back through the kitchen door.

Dirty dishes sat in the sink; clothes hung over the chair; a week's worth of mail and magazines lay strewn on the table.

Funny, she hadn't noticed them before. She heard Dave shuffling in another room and turned to follow him when a loud chattering drew her attention back toward the brush. A flurry of small black and yellow birds swooped and darted in front of her, chasing after each other like tiny dive bombers. Several of them settled into the sea-grape tree to preen their feathers. One of the largest birds began twittering and bobbing excitedly. It sidled up to another, tilted its head from one side to the other, and pecked around the other bird's beak as if kissing her.

Joanna stood still, watching, then shook her head and turned back toward the room where Dave waited. At the pile of clothes, she hesitated and lifted a t-shirt from the top, held it up in front of her and folded it. Then she placed it back on the pile, absently smoothing out the wrinkles as she did with Michael's shirts. She thought of him lying beside her that morning in bed, his body molded to the curve of her back, his arm thrown over her shoulder. She felt so safe and protected when they slept that way. It was one of the things that had made her fall in love with him. But now, it seemed like it was the only time he was affectionate. She felt a sudden pang, a yearning to feel that warmth again. She closed her eyes. A warm lethargy began to seep from her belly, radiating outward, filling her with a longing so intense she thought she might melt. But for which man? For Michael? For Dave? She sighed and continued around the table and through the doorway to the next room.

Dave sat on the bed, rolling a joint. Patting a spot next to him, he motioned for her to sit down. She did, leaving some room between them. Joanna pointed to a door on the other side of the room. "Does that go to the backyard, too?"

"Yup. Right from the bedroom, so you don't have to walk through the house from the shower." Dave handed her the joint. "You start the spleef, mahn." Chuckling, he lit a match.

Joanna brought the joint to her lips, placing her hand on his to steady the match, and drew a long breath. She coughed as a gush of smoke filled her lungs. Dave took the joint from her, and the sound of his deep draw hissed in her ears.

From the bed, she was close enough to touch the dresser, just inches from her left shoulder. Above the dresser, hung a mirror with several snapshots stuck to its frame. One shot showed Dave and another man standing on High Hat's porch. They grinned and raised their beer bottles in salute to the photographer. Another photo, one of an older man and woman with a young woman beside them, was propped upright on the dresser top in the kind of cardboard holder that comes with school portraits.

Joanna felt the slight pressure of Dave's fingers on her arm. She took the joint he offered. "Is that your family?" she asked.

"Sure, mahn."

She inhaled deeply and handed the joint back to him as she leaned forward to pick up the photo. The people all looked familiar but especially the young woman. Joanna looked at Dave, who was staring at her as if waiting for her reaction. His gaze made her blush, yet she found it hard to pull away. She dropped her eyes to the photo in her hands. "They look like they could be my relatives."

Dave laughed and handed her the spliff. "Maybe we were related in a past life. Here, smoke." He pointed to the young woman in the photo. "That's my sister. You sort of remind me of her." He shifted back on the bed. "I don't know. Maybe it's something about the way you talk. You don't really look like her. Weird, right?"

They were silent as they both studied the photo. He took a deep drag and held his breath, keeping the smoke in his lungs. When he spoke again, his voice came out half-croak, half-whisper. "Maybe that's why I feel like I know you, like we've been here before," he said, grinning.

"Oh, great! I remind you of your sister," Joanna said, with a half laugh. She rubbed a bit of dust from the photograph with her finger. "She doesn't look like you, either."

Dave shrugged.

Joanna stared at the young woman in the photo for a long time as they passed the joint back and forth. When she looked up again, the room had begun to glow pink from the reflection of the sun off the coral walls outside. A breeze rippled in warm waves through the window at the foot of the bed, and the dense air caught in Joanna's throat. The sounds of the compound were gone, and she imagined herself and Dave alone in a fishbowl, submerged and insulated from the outside world. His voice circled softly inside her head although he was not speaking, and she knew that they had been in this room, sitting together on this bed, many times before. She saw the future stretch out in front of them like a long, bright tunnel. Her heart began to pound. She seemed to rise on the warm rippling air, floating above the bed. She clutched Dave's arm.

"Hey, it's okay," he said, putting his hand on hers. "I'm not going anywhere." He offered her the joint. "Want another toke?"

The touch of his hand and the sound of his voice pulled her back into her body, and she felt the bed beneath her again. She shook her head and opened her mouth to speak, not really expecting anything to come out. "I was feeling a little spacy," she said and pulled her hand from his. She shook with the effort to control her nerves and broke into a series of short shivers in the hot room. "I guess I'm high enough. I get a little crazy if I get too high."

He licked his finger and wet the end of the joint, then slipped it into his pocket. "Good. Let's go sit outside. The fresh air will bring you down a little," he said, smiling.

He got up and edged past her to put the photo back on the dresser. She stood, waiting for him to go through the door to the kitchen, but instead he stepped back to let her pass in front of him. As she angled by him in the narrow space, he reached out to her but hesitated, holding his hand in mid-air, his fingers raised like a policeman halting traffic. He laughed and dropped his hand to his side. Joanna pretended not to see and slid past him.

The sun had fallen behind the tall sea-grape trees, so that the porch was now in shade. Two chairs faced the compound, their backs against the cinder block wall of the house, with a third by the railing. Joanna hesitated for a moment, then chose the chair farthest from the porch steps. Dave sat next to her, his feet propped on the other chair. "I like to sit like this and watch what's going on in the compound," he said, settling in.

Two little girls—Joanna guessed about eight—played with some dented pots and cups in front of the porch. One of the girls wore plastic sandals much too big for her. She walked around her friend and pretended to pour a liquid into the other girl's cup. The backs of the shoes stuck out at least three inches beyond her heels, smacking her feet as she walked, sounding like a pair of castanets. The girl looked at Dave, smiled. She poured an imaginary liquid into her own broken cup, lifted it to her mouth with a curved pinkie, and drank through pursed lips. Again, she smiled up at Dave.

"Quite the lady," Joanna said and laughed. She definitely felt better in the air. She moved her chair closer so she could put her feet up next to Dave's. A slight breeze blew, cooling the air around them. She arched her back and raised her arms to push the hair back from her forehead. She felt pleasantly high and full as if she had just finished a good meal. She was content to sit next to Dave, the two of them like some old married couple, watching the children play. "I think she's got a thing for you," Joanna said.

"Yeah, she likes to visit me." Dave watched the children as he spoke. "I gave her those sandals."

"That was nice of you."

"Well, I didn't actually give them to her. I threw them away because the strap broke." He turned toward Joanna. "They were cheap. Just a couple of dollars. She took them out of the trash and asked if she could have them." He put his feet on the floor and leaned forward with his elbows on his knees, moving closer to Joanna. "She actually pinned them together good enough so she could wear them. I never even considered fixing them. They were so cheap." He paused. Some flies buzzed around his head, distracting him. He swatted at them. "There's one kid who takes my old plastic shampoo bottles and uses them for buoys for his fishing lines. Things are more valuable here."

The children had finished their tea party and were jumping

rope.

"I have to admit, I get a kick out of having the kids around," Dave said.

"Do you have any?" Joanna asked.

"Not that I know of." He grinned and adjusted his feet on the chair. "How about you?"

"No. We've been waiting."

"For what?"

Joanna sighed and looked away. "I don't know. To get married, I guess." She shrugged. "We don't feel like we're ready yet."

"How long have you been together?"

"Nine years." Joanna picked at her nails. "But we met really young." For some reason, she felt like crying. She could feel the pressure building around her eyes. "We were only twenty."

"Yeah, that's pretty young. Too young, for true, mahn" Dave said.

Momma Samuel's voice flitted like a swallow through the air in search of the children as she sang out in patois, calling them to dinner. Her lilting summons seemed to vibrate inside Joanna, beckoning her as well. She rose from the chair to lean forward, following the scampering children with her eyes.

Dave stretched his arms behind his head. "All right! Food! Do you want to stay for dinner? Momma Samuel cooks for me. I'm sure she has enough for you."

Joanna sat down on the railing and smiled absently at Dave. Off to the right, in front of the kitchen shed, the children gathered around the pot where Momma Samuel ladled stew into their bowls. They jostled and bumped each other, laughing and jockeying to get closer to the pot. The sharp smell of pepper, the aroma of Jamaica, wafted to the porch. Joanna rubbed her nose and turned, resting her chin on her shoulder. She gazed down at the ground behind her as if captivated by something in the sandy dirt.

"I'd like you to stay," Dave said quietly.

She glanced at him and smiled, then stood up. She felt like she might just float away. "Michael's probably back," she said. "He probably wonders where I am." Joanna turned again toward the children as they sat eating their stew in a circle on the ground. The scene looked so idyllic that Joanna found herself wishing Michael were here to capture it with his camera. She shook her head and peered at Dave. "I guess I'd better be going. Thanks for the buzz. It was definitely what I needed to mellow out."

Dave bounded off his chair and stood in front of her, shifting from foot to foot, hands in pockets. "Hey, anytime," he said. He smiled down at his feet and then back at Joanna. They stood inches apart. For a brief moment, they seemed to sway towards each other, then away, like magnets attracting and repelling. Now it was Joanna's turn to inspect her feet. She glanced up at Dave, who was grinning a shy little-boy smile.

"Well, I've got to go," she said, wheeling around and jumping down the steps without waiting for him to answer.

"Hey," he called out, "maybe I'll come down tonight and check you guys out."

She hesitated a moment, her hand on the step railing, then smiled up at him. "Why not?"

***

The sun hung low on the horizon, mostly hidden behind the trees that lined the trail like a row of rustling guards. The day's last light bathed everything—the trees, the dust at her feet, the air, the clouds—with a warm, rosy glow, like a pastel watercolor. Michael, with his photographer's eye, had taught her to love the low, golden slant of the setting sun. These were the most beautiful moments of the day when the world was awash with a gentle softness, transmuted briefly into the alchemist's gold, before everything sank into the dull brown shadows of dusk and the dark hole of night.

She climbed a small incline, then walked down toward the spot where the path joined the trail back to the main road. She stopped, taking in the glimmering beauty of the sunset. As she watched, she began to cry softly, the tears running down her cheeks as fast as she could wipe them away. Was it the melancholy beauty of the approaching dusk or thoughts of Michael that made her cry? She didn't know. "Dumb," she muttered to herself and started again toward the main road, kicking a stone in front of her.

By the time she reached High Hat's, she had stopped crying. Michael was sitting on the porch, his feet propped on the railing, a Red Stripe in hand. He dropped his feet to the floor with a thud and raised the beer in a salute to her.

"How ya' doin'," he said, as cheerful as a salesman.

"I'm okay," she said and sat on the chair next to him. She didn't meet his gaze or smile.

"Where've you been? I've been here for hours!"

"I doubt it," she mumbled. She took off her sandals and dropped them to the floor, then began carefully massaging each foot, dusting the sand from them as she rubbed. He leaned over to help her brush the sand off, but she pushed his hand away.

"Did you take a walk?" he asked.

"Do you care?"

Michael was silent a moment, sipping his beer. "Hey, I was just asking. You said you were nervous and wanted to take a walk, so I thought maybe you did."

"I didn't want to take a walk alone. You knew that. So, where were you?" She shot the words at him, then grabbed his beer and took a long drink.

"You want one?" he asked, avoiding her question. "I'll get it for you."

"I'll drink this one. You get another."

He ambled into the bar room and ordered a beer from High Hat. His voice sounded measured, smooth, even carefree as he joked with the bartender. He came back out and handed a beer to Joanna. A familiar reggae song floated from the bar, mixing with the music of the patois of the men who lounged inside. A cool, blue-grey twilight settled over the road and the sea beyond. A breeze, tasting of salt, blew softly over them.

"You have no reason to be mad at me, you know," Michael

said. When Joanna didn't answer, he went on. "This is a vacation. We're supposed to be having fun." He leaned his elbows on his knees and looked at Joanna, profiled in the light from the bar. "I mean, when did you ever see a bunch of guys moving a whole shack down the street by hand? How could I miss that?"

"You could have gotten hurt, and I didn't have a key," she said, staring into the darkening grayness.

"Get real, Jo. You weren't thinking about me getting hurt. You were pissed because I left you."

Joanna jerked around, glaring in the dim light. "That's not true. I was worried … OK, mad, too. And we're supposed to be working on our relationship, not you running off alone." She took a gulp of her Red Stripe.

"Jo, it was fun. You should have come with me."

"You're crazy. It was dangerous!"

A car roared past on the road, its muffler dragging and clanging underneath, for a few moments drowning out the reggae from the bar. When it was past, Joanna said, "Besides, you didn't give a shit if I was with you or not."

Michael shifted in his chair but remained silent. Joanna could feel the tension building inside her, ready to start the flow of tears again as the silence grew.

Finally, he said, "It's not that. It's just that we don't have to do everything together. I wanted to do it, and I knew you wouldn't go, so I just did it."

Joanna inspected a mosquito bite on her arm. The juke box inside the bar was quiet as a new reggae song dropped onto the turntable. In the stillness, the hiss of the ocean whispered over the porch. Joanna could see Michael's silhouette in the dwindling light but couldn't make out his expression. "You used to want me to do things with you," she said.

"I still want you to do things with me."

As if in response to his words, a burst of laughter exploded from the bar and rushed over their heads out into the darkness.

"Great," Joanna said, looking over her shoulder.

"Come on, Jo." His voice took on a soothing tone. "It's just that we don't have to do everything together."

"I heard you the first time."

Two Jamaicans swaggered out of the bar and down the porch steps, weaving together as if reggaeing their way towards the road. Their motions were easy, languid, rippling like waves rolling back to the sea, and soon they were lost to the blackness of the road, only their voices lingering like faint music from a distant radio. The jukebox had paused again, and the slapping of the sea sounded to Joanna like a giant hand clapping. They were both quiet, listening, each lost in their own thoughts.

Joanna so wanted to believe they still had a chance. But did they really? They had tried counseling, but it didn't go well. At their last session, Michael had blurted out, "See what I have to deal with? I'm tired of always having to take care of her." His words had felt like a slap in the face. But later, on the drive home, he had tried to make it up to her. "You know, maybe we should forget about the counseling, just try to work it out ourselves. Now that Reggae's gone, we could go back to Jamaica. We both love it there. We would have a lot of time alone."

And so, they had come back. Joanna felt Michael's touch on her arm. "Are you hungry?" he asked.

The music from the bar started up again. Bob Marley crooned, "No woman no cry." It felt like he was singing to her, and Joanna softened at the words. She smiled at Michael. "Yeah, a little hungry."

"Let's get changed and go eat." Michael stood in front of her and took her hand. "Come on, we'll have some dinner and not be mad anymore."

Joanna looked up at him as he towered above her, her eyes wet with tears. "I love you, Michael."

"I know, babe," he said, and drew her up to kiss her lightly on the lips. "Don't worry. We'll be all right." He slipped his arm around her waist. They walked into the building and down the long hallway lit by a single bare, orange bulb. Once inside they tiptoed and edged around each other like visitors to a sickroom, neither wanting to upset the delicate truce between them. The sound of reggae echoed through the room, a thumping beat in the bed, along the floor, and even in the bathroom, where it seemed to pour from the pipes with the water.

Michael collapsed on the bed, his legs stretched out in front of him. "You know, it's really not good for you to be so dependent on me," he said, his face a cheerful mask.

"I know, Michael. We've been through this before."

"Yeah, Jo, but it's true."

Joanna sat down on the edge of the bed. "Do you think I like being dependent on you? It makes me feel like I can't take care of myself."

He reached out and touched her shoulder. "Well, you've got to find other interests or something, you know, maybe other friends."

"How am I going to do that down here?" She shifted her weight and moved farther back onto the bed so that Michael had to move his legs.

"I don't mean in Jamaica," he said, "I mean back home."

"I don't know, Michael. It's not like I don't have any friends."

The pounding bass from the music next door beat in rhythm with her heart, drumming inside her chest like a tiny thumping hammer. It was as if the heartbeat of the island kept time with her own.

Michael watched her and shifted positions. His leg began that familiar jiggle. Keeping his voice low, he said, "Maybe, when we get home, Jo, we should think some more about trying an open relationship."

She winced and spun around to glare at him, the muscles of her throat taut as ropes. He raised his hands as if to ward off a blow. "Hey, we've talked about this before," he said.

It was true they sometimes joked about an open relationship, discussing which of their friends they found attractive and who might make a good bed partner. They tried to be open about their feelings although often Joanna found Michael's honesty painful.

Joanna stared at her hands. "I know we've talked about an

open relationship, but never really seriously, and never when we weren't getting along. It's always been more like a fantasy, hasn't it? I mean, are you bored or something?"

"It's not that, Jo. It's just that I can't be with you every single minute, and there are things we don't like to do together. So maybe if you could find other people to hang out with—it wouldn't have to be lovers, it could just be friends—then I wouldn't feel so responsible for you all the time."

Joanna cringed and shot up from the bed. "Well, I'm sorry you feel so damned responsible—*all the time.*"

"Jo, sit down." He pulled her back down to the bed and put his arm around her. "You said yourself it might be fun to try it some time. Maybe you wouldn't feel so dependent. We can think about it, anyway, can't we? Will you?"

"It doesn't sound like such a good idea right now," she said.

"Just think about it, okay?" He pulled her towards him until she was lying by his side.

"I love you," he said, "That's what's important."

"I don't know, Michael. I just don't know."

CHAPTER FOUR

The sun beat down on the cliffs, turning the air into a steam bath. Dave had met them earlier for breakfast at High Hat's, and they had decided to spend the day at the cliff-side cottages of his friend Kevin. After breakfast, they had changed quickly into bathing suits and walked the mile up the road to the cliffs.

Three cottages nestled among a cluster of tall, umbrella-like palms. Strands of gray moss hung languidly from sagging limbs, almost touching the ground. The trees cast a melancholy air as if the weight of the moss were too much to bear.

Kevin lived in the smallest of the cottages with his two German shepherds. The dogs looked out of place here with their thick coats hanging from bodies wasted by the heat. Both shepherds walked with such a pronounced sway—hip problems, Kevin said—that Joanna thought they might keel over. She held out her hand to them, but the dogs turned and meandered back to pant under the large, drooping trees.

Kevin, too, was lean, perhaps a little too thin like his dogs. His body was bare to the sun except for a pair of cut-off jeans that slipped below the line of his deep, reddish-gold tan, exposing a swath of lighter skin. He rented two of the cottages to tourists at exorbitant prices, which they willingly paid for the privilege of being removed from other tourists.

"Only one cottage is rented now," he said, with the slightest twang. He spoke in a lazy drawl as if he, too, might prefer lying in the shade with the dogs. He told them to help themselves to the lounge chairs by the water and retired to the palms.

Dave steered Joanna and Michael along a concrete walkway that led through jagged rock to a small shelter thatched above with palms and open to the air on all sides. Joanna stopped in the cool shade to feel the ocean breeze against her skin as the men walked on. She glanced over the wide expanse of gray rock that extended uninterrupted on either side of the walkway. The exposed rock jutted up, stone hard, and razor sharp. Joanna flinched at the thought of slipping onto the uninviting surface.

Something fluttered and caught Joanna's eye. In the distance, a boy and a girl fished off the cliff, the girl's skirt waving in the wind. Joanna wondered how they could have walked on the serrated surface of the rock. She shook her head. Maybe they weren't really there. Maybe the weed had her imagining things again. She rubbed her eyes, then started down the path.

Dave and Michael had followed the walkway to another paved area where half a dozen chairs looked out over the ocean. She joined the men at the metal ladder that dropped from its anchor in the concrete to the clear water five feet below. Michael was already donning snorkeling gear.

"You coming?" Dave asked.

Michael, she noticed, was more interested in his gear than in her, but she wasn't really surprised. She turned to Dave and smiled. "No, not yet. I like to get good and sweaty before I go in," she said, sitting down on a chaise lounge. She searched in her bag for her suntan lotion and began to rub it on her arms.

Michael flapped awkwardly toward the cliff's edge, like a giant frog. He pulled his snorkel from his mouth long enough to say, "Here I go," then jumped into the ocean. Joanna and Dave watched as Michael began to snorkel. Dave turned to Joanna. "Need some help with that suntan oil? I can put some on your back."

She handed the tube to him. "Is he okay alone in the water?" she asked.

Dave glanced toward Michael. "Yeah, he's fine. Looks happy as a fish in there. No sharks around here." He smiled. "Here, turn around." Squeezing some onto his palm, he rubbed it between his hands and began smoothing it into her skin. "How's that feel?"

"Nice."

"Good." He bent close enough to kiss her shoulder, but instead, ran his hand along the curve of her neck. "Now, get nice and hot, okay?"

She stopped his hand with her own and smiled. "I will. Now, you go cool off."

"Touché." He laughed, snorkeled up, and jumped in the water.

She finished spreading the lotion on her legs and lay back to bake. The sun's glare seeped through her eyelids, and its heat spread from the surface of her skin downward throughout her body. It seemed to concentrate below her belly until she couldn't tell if the heat was coming from outside or from deep inside her. She retreated under the orange canopy of her eyelids, weaving in and out of a sparkling dream. She sank deeper and deeper into the brightness, feeling herself shrinking until she seemed tiny enough to float in the warm, thick liquid of her own womb. Somewhere far away she heard the sea lapping at the rocks. The gentle sound led her deeper into a molten dream where she drifted with the tides, floating just the other side of consciousness in a hot ocean. The hiss of the sea enveloped her until the sound took form, seemed to call her name, became an insistent whisper. She opened her eyes and nearly jumped from the chair. Jeevan squatted next to her, murmuring softly into her ear.

"Jeevan, you scared the shit out of me."

He laughed. "How yuh gettin' so scared, mahn? Ah no hurt yuh. Ah come to beg a question." Rocking back on his haunches, he sat down on the chair next to Joanna. She shaded her eyes and inspected his chartreuse pants, purple t-shirt, and the stars and stripes of his knitted cap. His clothes looked as if a kid had picked them out, but somehow the effect was endearing. She shook her head, clucking.

"Whad's de matter, mahn?" he asked.

The smooth brown skin of his face gave him a cherubic look, making her want to stroke his cheek. She took a few breaths.

"Nothing," she said. "The sun's in my eyes. What did you want to ask me?"

He slid his sunglasses down from his forehead to cover his eyes, guarding them from Joanna. Then he swung his legs up onto a chaise lounge and settled in as if planning to stay awhile. He turned to her with what could only be described as a shit-eating grin. "Yuh must taste some nice Jamaican cock," he said.

Joanna's eyes snapped wide open. She couldn't possibly have heard him right. She concentrated on breathing slowly and tried to control the quivering of her voice. "What did you say?"

The grin was gone, his eyes dark holes behind the sunglasses. "Yuh wanna taste some Jamaican cock, mahn?"

Joanna looked around for Michael and Dave, snorkeling face down about twenty feet off the cliff. She calculated whether she could get to the water before Jeevan caught her. He was grinning again. She stood up, her heart pounding so hard in her chest she was sure he could see it. "Jeevan, are you crazy?"

He pushed the sunglasses onto his forehead and looked as if she had insulted him. "No, mahn," he said, dropping his eyes to his hands. "Ah just axin' yuh and yuh mahn and Dave to come eat dinner wid me and the woman."

It seemed to Joanna as if he were speaking another language. Was it patois? The air around him took on the orange shimmer of her sun dream. The waves splashed and echoed like the hollow sound of the sea in a seashell. She felt as if she were rising into the sky. She grabbed at her chair. And then one of the German shepherds barked. The illusion passed, and she stared at Jeevan. "Did you just invite us to come to dinner at your house?"

Jeevan stared at the dog, then back at her with the most earnest eyes as if she held his fate in her hands. "True, mahn. Sure, mahn. Ah tellin' yuh, de rooster, 'im get killed dis mornin' by de motorcycle, mahn. Dis bird plenty plenty mean all de time. 'Im chase me and everybody dat visit me dooryard. Plenty mean, mahn. But now him dead, Ah feel dis bird meat mek very good eatin'." He beamed like a kid.

Joanna's mouth dropped open. "Jeevan, you bastard!" She

picked up a towel and threw it at him. He lunged and caught it in mid-air, chuckling.

"You did ask me if I wanted to taste Jamaican cock! You prick!"

"Ah jokin' wid yuh, mahn, dat's all. Good joke, true? Yuh t'ink me ax yuh somet'ing else, right? Ah feel yuh strivin' to understand me, but yuh can't do so. Ah jokin' wid yuh, mahn."

She glared at him a moment longer, then began laughing. "You bastard," she said. "I can't believe you did that."

"Dis a good joke, right?"

"Yeah, very funny." She sat down on the edge of the chaise lounge. "Are you serious about us coming for dinner?"

"Yeh, mahn. Yuh all t'ree must come, dis night, for sure, mahn."

"Well, that's nice of you, Jeevan. Really nice of your wife to cook for us."

Jeevan's eyes clouded over, and again, he looked insulted, or maybe angry, Joanna couldn't tell. "'Im not me wife, mahn. 'Im me woman fer now, dat's all."

Joanna tilted her head and stared at him, puzzled. "Okay," she said after a bit. "What time should we come?"

"Yuh must tell me de time."

"Well, what time's good for your woman?"

He spit on the concrete. "Dat don't matter, mahn. Yuh must tell me."

It mattered to Joanna, but she couldn't very well argue with him when he was inviting them to his house. She sighed and said, "Six is good for us."

He rose to leave. "Too late, mahn. Yuh must come at five." He turned and sauntered back toward the cottages without saying good-bye.

***

When they arrived at Jeevan's, a little after five, he was sitting on his front stoop, rolling a spliff. The house was little more than a shack, but by now Joanna was no longer shocked by the poverty in Jamaica. Jeevan's home was constructed with uniform planks instead of the usual slabs of mismatched, salvaged wood. That made it a cut above most Joanna had seen, except, of course, for Momma Samuel's. The roof was a patchwork jumble of old shingles, pieces of tin, and plastic tiles. White curtains fluttered at the screened windows adding a woman's touch. His woman's doing, thought Joanna. The doorway where Jeevan sat gaped wide open.

Chickens scattered in every direction as Joanna and the men made their way toward Jeevan. He didn't greet them but sat licking the spliff to seal it. Joanna could see right through the front door of the shack to the backyard. She caught a glimpse of a woman's brightly flowered dress through the backdoor. Without turning his head, Jeevan called out to the woman. She appeared at the back door carrying a baby on her hip. She stepped up and disappeared like a phantom into the shadow of the shack, emerging again at the front door to stand behind Jeevan. She was a plump woman with an inviting softness to her smooth, cocoa-brown flesh. The baby, a miniature of Jeevan, showed the same softness in his chubby little arms and legs. To Joanna, they looked like a Madonna and child.

Jeevan didn't acknowledge the woman and child with even a turn of the head. Instead, speaking to Michael and Dave, he nodded toward her, "Dis me woman. Tell de mahn yuh name, girl."

She smiled shyly, showing missing front teeth. In a barely audible whisper, she said, "Dahlia. De baby name Christopher."

At that Jeevan smiled and turned toward the child. Taking hold of the baby's bare foot, he said, "Yeh, dat me son, for true. 'Im growing big." Dropping the boy's foot, he nudged Dahlia's knee with his elbow. She turned and retreated through the house and out the back door while Jeevan stood up. "Ah feel is best we sit inside de house, mahn, if we plannin' smoke dis spleef. Come," he said, turning and stepping up to enter.

Dave motioned Joanna to go in and held her hand as she took the high step from the ground into the house. He stepped into the house himself as Michael followed behind.

"No helping hand for me?" Michael said, laughing.

"Sure," Dave said, extending his hand. Michael took it and pulled himself up.

Joanna watched from inside, wondering what Dave must think of Michael's comment. She shrugged and turned to look around the shack. The inside walls were plastered with yellowing newspapers. Joanna could see through the planks of the floor to the dirt below. A Formica-topped table dominated the room. Three vinyl chairs circled it, looking a little worse for wear. An arrangement of plastic flowers stood in an empty beer bottle in the center of the lacy plastic tablecloth. To the right, a doorway led to what looked like a tiny bedroom. A bureau, cluttered with bottles, filled one whole wall. The headboard of a bed stuck out into the doorway, the rest of it hidden, obviously too big for the small space.

Jeevan sat on a wooden box and motioned for his guests to take the three chairs. There was barely enough room for all of them to fit around the table without touching the walls behind them. The place reminded Joanna of a child's playhouse. The entire shack would fit into her living room at home. A pang of guilt jolted her, and for a moment, it hit her how rich she was compared to Jeevan and Dahlia. But her thoughts were quickly distracted by Jeevan offering the spliff.

They passed the joint around the table while Michael and Dave launched into a description of their snorkeling adventures. As the marijuana seeped into Joanna's brain, the men's talk seemed to subside into a monotonous drone. Outside, the clatter of pans and the murmuring of the baby took on the quality of a familiar reggae song. It seemed to beckon to Joanna. As ganja smoke swirled all around her, the men's voices felt dull and heavy, weighing her down. Joanna shook her head to clear their words from her ears and rose to go out back.

"Where yuh go, mahn?" Jeevan asked.

"I thought I'd talk to Dahlia."

"'Im don't matter, yuh know, mahn." Jeevan's eyebrows knit into a scowl.

Joanna spun to face him. "Really? Well, I feel like talking to her."

He glared at her, holding her with his eyes, reaching deep inside her. Her knees went weak, and for no rational reason, she felt ashamed, as if Jeevan had caught her in a lie. Michael shifted uncomfortably in his chair, briefly distracting Jeevan, who glanced away, but Joanna kept her eyes on Jeevan as if held in a spell until Dave spoke.

"Oh, let her go, mahn," Dave said. "They like to talk women's talk."

Jeevan shrugged and smiled at Joanna. His smile washed over her, releasing her. Freed, she turned to step down into the backyard. Outside, Dahlia looked up from the pot she was stirring. A slight smile played on her lips. Before Joanna could return the lukewarm welcome, the woman looked down again. Dahlia held Christopher on one hip, her muscular arm wrapped around his waist, as she deftly mixed with the other hand. She reached up with the spoon in hand and tucked a tuft of hair into her colorful bandana.

She cooked under a metal roof attached to the shack, propped up by poles at the corners. The stove was primitive, a simple series of pipes and tubes, two burners, and a glass container half-filled with an amber liquid. The acrid odor of kerosene mixed with the spicy aromas of the food. A rusted drum filled with dark water, squatted next to a rickety table with a chipped enamel basin, its blue, speckled surface riddled with brown cracks. Joanna wondered if it could still hold water. Beyond the cooking shed, vegetation grew to within a short distance of the shed, dense enough to hide any other houses nearby. A path led into the bush from the backyard.

Joanna turned to Dahlia and bent to inhale the steam rising from the pot. "Smells good," she said. "What are you cooking?" Dahlia looked amused. Joanna tried again, pointing in the pot. "What's in the pot?"

Dahlia grinned like a schoolgirl with a secret. "Cock," she said.

Joanna started for an instant, then laughed. Dahlia joined her, and they giggled like teenagers. "The rooster who got killed by the motorcycle, right?" Joanna asked.

Dahlia nodded and juggled the baby higher on her hip.

"Would you like me to hold him?" Joanna held her hands out to the baby. He reached toward her as Dahlia leaned forward. The baby grabbed for Joanna, but her arms sagged under his unexpected weight. Dahlia reached out to keep him from falling as Joanna recovered and planted him on her own hip. Both women laughed again.

"'Im big boy," said Dahlia, looking proudly at the child, who tugged at the bead necklace around Joanna's neck. His mother reached out and swatted his hand away from the jewelry.

"He certainly is." Joanna bounced him on her hip, making him gurgle. She had to use both arms to support the child and marveled at his mother's strength. "You are a big boy, aren't you, Christopher?" she said, kissing him on his soft, chubby cheek.

Dahlia reached into a paper bag on the ground by her bare feet and pulled out a slender red pepper. She picked up a knife from the table, then held the blade up straight. "Plenty sharp," she said with a chuckle and stuck her thumb close to Joanna's face. "T'umb very t'ick. See?" It was covered with a tough callus like a construction worker's. She smiled and began slicing the pepper against her thumb, cutting it down the middle and carefully discarding the seeds hidden inside. "Seed too hot," she said and dropped the diced pieces into the stew. She pulled a can of condensed milk from a cupboard hanging above the stove, stirred the liquid into the pot and looked at Joanna. Her gaze grew mischievous, like a child considering a prank. "Jeevan say yuh friends long time. 'Im say yuh bin Jamaica plenty times. 'Im say he know yuh good."

Joanna shifted Christopher to her other hip, absently wondering what he must weigh. She turned back to Dahlia. "Yeah, Michael and I met Jeevan on our first trip to Jamaica. He sold us ganja." She laughed. "Very powerful ganja."

Dahlia sniffed as if smelling some foul odor. "'Im say yuh plenty pretty lady."

Christopher reached again for Joanna's necklace. Dahlia knocked his hand away again, this time so close to Joanna's chin that she had to turn her head. She backed up a step. "It's okay. He can touch it if he wants," Joanna said. She wasn't sure how to respond to Dahlia's comment. Was Dahlia jealous? She and Michael had known Jeevan for all of five weeks all together.

"Where yuh must get de money come Jamaica?" Dahlia said. "Ah feel yuh got plenty money come to Jamaica so much times."

For an instant, Joanna saw an image of her own apartment superimposed over the rough shack before her. Guilt swept over her again, made heavier by the weight of the baby in her arms. And for an instant, it was clear that she was responsible for the poverty in which Dahlia and her baby lived, as if Joanna's very existence were somehow the cause. She shook her head. Crazy, she thought. She looked at Dahlia and tried to sound breezy. "Well, it does cost a lot to come here, but lots of people in the States have more money than we do." Joanna reddened, embarrassed by her silly attempt to justify herself.

Dahlia reached for a saltshaker on the table beside Joanna and began tapping salt into the stew. Without meeting Joanna's eyes, she said, "Nobody gettin' big money here. Ah doan even 'ave de money to buy de boy 'im medicine."

Joanna felt Dahlia's words like a jab in her gut. "What medicine? What's the matter with him?" Joanna's arms began to ache, and she wondered how much longer she could support the baby's weight.

"De doctor say 'im need de vit ... a ... mahns," Dahlia said, "to mek 'im plenty strong."

The baby looked healthy to Joanna. He certainly felt healthy. Did he really need vitamins? Was Dahlia playing her? Making a game out of getting money from her? Still, she felt some dark, vague sense of responsibility, like she owed some long-standing debt to Dahlia and her baby. And it was true that it wouldn't break her to buy a bottle of vitamins for the baby, either.

"Where Ah must get de money from? Maybe Ah get it from yuh?" Dahlia said, lowering her eyes.

Joanna frowned as a rustle in the bushes caught her attention. Happy for an excuse to ignore Dahlia's question, she switched the baby to her other hip and walked towards the path she had noticed earlier. She took a few steps but stopped when the path turned and cut off her view of the house. "Where does the path lead?" she asked Dahlia, as she walked back to the shed. Dahlia glared at her, but Joanna kept smiling. Moving the baby higher on her hip, she pulled one arm from under him and pointed to the path. "Where does it go?" she asked again, ignoring Dahlia's look.

Dahlia went back to her stirring. "Dat way de toilet. Yuh must go dere?"

"No, no. I'm good. Thanks," Joanna said.

Dahlia's face went slack, and her eyes rose under hooded lids to look past Joanna at the door frame where Jeevan stood above them.

"Yuh like de boy?" he said to Joanna. "Yuh want one like 'im, too?" He laughed.

Joanna turned to Dahlia at a loss for how to answer. Dahlia stared into the pot, intent on shaking some new spice into the simmering mix.

"He's very cute," Joanna said and moved the baby back again to her other hip. "And big, too!"

"'Im too big for yuh. Yuh such a little t'ing." Jeevan hurled something in patois at Dahlia. The woman looked up at him, then moved to take the baby from Joanna. Again, Jeevan said something Joanna couldn't quite make out, but his angry tone was clear.

This time Dahlia glowered and banged her spoon against the metal pot. "Soon come, mahn. Doan worry wid dat. Soon come." She turned up the flame under the pan until it shot up the sides.

Jeevan reached down, and taking Joanna's hand, hoisted her up the high step into the house. "Yuh must come bahk inside," he said and led her to her chair. "Dinner soon come."

Joanna sat down at the table. She noticed that Jeevan had moved her chair, so she was closer to the box he was sitting on. Michael handed her the joint. "What were you two talking about?"

"Not much. The baby mostly," Joanna answered, coughing on the smoke from the spliff. "Michael, do you have those Red Stripes we brought? I could use something to drink."

Michael rummaged in the backpack at his feet and brought out a beer for each of them. Jeevan reached behind him to take several dishes from a low hutch, passing them around the table with four spoons. Then he grabbed three mugs and handed them out, keeping a plastic cup for himself. "Here, yuh must use dese for dis special dinner." He looked almost grim as if this was indeed a solemn occasion.

Soon Dahlia came to the back door and set the child down on the floor, then disappeared back into the yard. The baby toddled over to Jeevan, who lifted him onto his lap. With the baby on his knee, Jeevan's whole appearance softened. He cooed and played with his son, poking him in his round belly and tickling him under his arms. The child giggled and cooed back, clearly delighted with the attention.

Dahlia appeared at the door again, this time placing the pot on the floor before hoisting herself into the room. She bent over stiffly like a woman wearing a tight girdle and picked the pot up off the floor. Circling the table, she dished out the stew with a large ladle, her soft flesh pressing into their arms and backs in the tiny space. Joanna felt awkward with another woman waiting on her and the men, but there was so little room it didn't make sense to try and help. When Dahlia was finished serving, she set the pot on the hutch behind Jeevan and took the baby from him. Taking a bowl from the shelf, she helped herself to some stew with one hand and, still holding the child, padded into the bedroom to sit on the bed while the others ate at the table.

Joanna looked from one man to the other. She couldn't believe that Dahlia was actually planning to eat in the bedroom, like some servant. She caught Michael's eye who returned her pained look with one that said he was as uncomfortable as she. But Dave and Jeevan seemed oblivious as they dug into the stew on their plates. Joanna looked toward the bedroom and called out, "Dahlia, why don't you come in here and sit on this chair. Michael and I can share one."

No answer came back. Jeevan looked up briefly, then went back to his stew as Joanna turned to him. "Why doesn't Dahlia come eat with us? I could even sit on the hutch. I don't mind."

Jeevan held his spoon in mid-air and looked wide-eyed at Joanna. "Sit on de hutch! No, mahn, dat would truly shame me, mahn," he said, pouting. He nudged Michael with his hand, still holding the spoon. "Ah feel yuh must tell yuh wife to leave it, mahn, and eat de dinner. Dis good Jamaican cock," he said, pointing at his plate and laughing. He dipped his spoon in again and began to eat, smiling broadly at Joanna with his mouth brimming.

Michael shrugged and started in again on a discussion of some fish he had seen while snorkeling. Joanna pushed the food around on her plate, her appetite gone. She wanted to get up and sit with Dahlia, but something warned her not to, a sense that she might not understand all the dynamics of the situation, a feeling that she might be insulting not only Jeevan but Dahlia with her actions. Besides, her exchange with Dahlia in the backyard had made her uneasy. She felt a gentle tap against her foot under the table and looked up to see Dave watching her. He smiled and nodded toward her plate. She began to eat, reluctantly at first, but then with relish, as the hot, savory taste of the Jamaican chicken filled her mouth.

When the meal was over, they smoked another spliff while Dahlia stayed in the bedroom, nursing the baby. In a few minutes, she wandered back into the front room, the baby crawling before her, and began to clear the dishes. Joanna rose to help her, hoping Dahlia would understand her actions as a peace offering. "Dahlia, the stew was really good, but hot!" she said as they worked.

The Jamaican woman smiled, "Yeh, mahn, Jamaican food very hot, for true. Mek yuh sweat. Mek yuh cool."

Joanna felt the tension between them lessen. She was following Dahlia out back with the dishes when Jeevan called to her. "Yuh must sit and drink some rum wid us," he said, pulling a bottle from the hutch and setting it with a bang on the table. Dahlia took the dishes from Joanna and motioned for her to sit down.

Jeevan had the baby on his lap and was bouncing him up and down on his knee while the boy squealed. He stopped and handed the baby a spoon. "Sunday much big day for Christopher," he said. "Is 'im baptism day." He took the spoon from the baby and began tapping it playfully on the child's hand. "Michael, mahn, yuh must come to the baptism."

Michael looked as if someone had invited him to a funeral. He hated churches. Joanna almost laughed at the distressed look on his face. Dave sat grinning.

Jeevan ignored Michael's lack of enthusiasm. "Yuh must bring yuh camera wid, mahn, and shoot de pictures of de baptism."

Michael smiled, noticeably relieved. "Sure, man, I can do that for you. I'll take photos."

"Mudder," Jeevan called, putting the baby down and giving him a gentle shove towards the back door.

Dahlia appeared just in time to sweep him up. She looked at Joanna. "Yuh must come, too, lady. Mek big honor for de boy den."

Taken aback, Joanna stammered, "Wow, thanks, Dahlia, ... I'd love to come." She felt a warm flush come over her as the rum slithered down her throat. The combination of weed, food, and the rum blended together to send Joanna into a dream-like state. She understood suddenly that, somehow, this baptism was a major event in her own life, as if destiny, like a giant wave, had carried her to this place at this very time just so she could play a part in this child's baptism. She sensed a deep connection, again, like she had known this woman and her child all her life. No, that was silly. Dahlia was just being polite. Yet something heavy settled in the pit of Joanna's stomach. She reached slowly toward her glass of rum, concentrating on it as if an answer lay submerged there.

Jeevan's voice broke into her reverie. "Dave, yuh must come, too, for true, mahn."

Dave took a sip of rum and settled back in his chair. "Thanks, man, but I might have to take some tourists out Sunday."

"Is okay, mahn. No bodderation if yuh can no do so." Jeevan poured another round of rum, and they sat around the table long enough to finish the bottle. Dahlia and the baby were nowhere to be seen as if they had melted into the twilight of the approaching night. At around ten, the men and Joanna smoked another joint, then with thanks to Jeevan, the three Americans set out for the bar at the Paradise.

CHAPTER FIVE

Joanna walked between Michael and Dave as they ambled down the road towards the roundabout at the center of town. Her head still swirled from the mix of rum and weed. With each step, she hesitated. Somehow, gravity had reversed direction and was pushing her foot up. The streetlights, scattered at random along the road, deepened the darkness between the posts. But Joanna felt secure between Michael and Dave. It felt so familiar to walk with them to the Paradise as if the three of them had walked together through the Jamaican night many times before. She wanted to take both of them by the arm, pulling them toward her so she could lift her feet off the ground and let them carry her like a little girl. She thought about what it would be like to live in a house with both of them. She saw the three of them sitting around her kitchen table at home, drinking beer. The image was so real that she stopped short. "Dave, you should come visit us at home when we all get back."

The men went on a few steps before they realized she had stopped. In the dim light, Joanna couldn't see their faces clearly. They appeared as dark shadows. The sea whispered as she stood still waiting for an answer.

Dave's voice came like an echo of that whisper. "I'm not sure, man. I hardly ever leave here. I really don't know when I'll be back in the States."

She felt a momentary pang, a slight jab at her heart, and started toward the men. "Oh, you know." She laughed. "Just an idea. I guess I was in the ozone. Spacing out. You know?" She hoped that neither of the men could read her thoughts.

The lights of the Paradise glowed on the road ahead of them as music tumbled from the bar's open windows. As they turned into the dooryard and approached the door, Joanna felt as if a hand were pushing her back toward the darkness of the road. She fell behind the men and watched as they climbed the steps to the bar. The light from the doorway shone on their faces, but from where she stood, she saw only their backs. They were two dark figures outlined against the bright mouth of the entrance, indistinguishable from each other. For a moment, she couldn't tell which was Michael and which was Dave.

As the men stepped into the light, they were swallowed up, plucked from above by some gigantic hand. She was seized by a wave of nausea that almost buckled her knees. She gasped, unable to get enough of the hot, soggy air into her lungs. The reggae from the bar stopped, and she knew she was the only person in the entire world. Was she dying? Did Dahlia put something in the stew? Some voodoo drug? She clutched at her chest. Should she call Michael? She knew he would tell her it was just nerves. He'd say, walk. Yes, she should walk. She would be okay if she walked. Moving was good.

She straightened up and forced herself to concentrate on breathing slowly. If she could get to the bar, get to Michael, it would be all right. She tried to move her legs, but she couldn't. Some force held her feet cemented to the ground. She wanted to scream, but nothing came out. She was trapped in a silent nightmare.

But, then Dave called to her. "What's the matter? Are you coming?"

As if jolted by an electric current, she felt her feet set free. "I ..." She stopped, wondering what she could say that wouldn't sound crazy. "I just wanted to ... you know, get myself together," she managed to stammer.

"Hey, Babe, you look great. Come on." He came down the steps, took her hand, and helped her up.

Michael lounged at an empty table and motioned to them. She followed Dave to the table, still in a bit of a daze. She felt as if she had returned from the land of the dead only to be deposited in the middle of a wild party. Reggae blared from a jukebox. Couples danced on a tiny, wooden floor at the rear of the bar. Red and yellow lights flashed across the chrome top of a jukebox like brightly colored insects chasing each other while beneath the domed cover a rack of records waited patiently for their turn. Joanna stared captivated as the mechanical arm moved along the row of records, hesitated briefly, contemplating its choice, then picked out a record to drop it beneath the curved stylus. It was a relic from the American fifties, and it looked both out of place and perfectly at home in this Jamaican bar.

Michael rose to go to the bar, but just then, the waitress came over, planting herself in front of him. He sat back down heavily. She was in her mid-twenties, attractive, sweetly plump, and wearing jeans so tight that she could barely bend her knees when she walked. She wore a white halter with a deep V neck that exposed the cleavage of her breasts. She lazed by their table as if content to wait all night for them to make up their minds. They ordered drinks, and she disappeared among a group of men gathered at the bar.

Joanna turned to the dancers. They undulated slowly to the reggae, like seaweed moving to underwater currents. One couple, clearly tourists, stood out among the others, their movements jerky, almost spasmodic, as if they were dancing to some unknown beat in their heads. They looked so out of place. She touched Michael's arm. "Do you want to dance?"

He put his hand over hers and smiled. "Not yet. I need a drink first." He shifted in his chair to look around the room. "Where's that waitress? Dave, why don't you dance with Joanna while I go get the waitress?" He got up and walked toward the bar.

Joanna frowned at Michael's retreating back, then turned toward Dave, who grinned, clearly pleased to find himself alone with her. She couldn't make up her mind whether to be angry at Michael's brush-off or happy with the chance to dance with Dave.

Dave shrugged. "Wanna dance?"

Screw Michael, she thought. "Why not?"

Joanna led him to an empty space on the floor where she could watch the bar. She found Michael easily in the crowd of dark faces. She tried to keep her eyes on him as he stood at the bar, talking with their waitress. She had turned to face him at the crowded bar so that her breasts practically touched his chest. They both smiled, and Michael seemed to be describing something to her. He stretched his arm and hand out over the bar as if to point to something far away. Joanna watched, anger churning inside her. But she couldn't help but be distracted by Dave's body so close to hers, and soon she drifted into a soft, dream-like space as they moved to the music.

Suddenly the room got quiet. Only Michael continued to gesture and talk, oblivious to the change. A Jamaican man in a Yankees' cap detached himself from the crowd at the far end of the bar and stood watching Michael and the waitress. The woman looked past Michael toward the man in the cap, and as Michael turned to look behind him, the man, in what seemed like a single motion, strode over to Michael and jammed a knife into the bar next to Michael's hand. Only the music of the jukebox filled the silence.

"Don't mess wid yuh life, mahn," the Jamaican said, bringing his face close to Michael's. "Dat me woman, yuh know, mahn."

Michael turned ashen under his tan. "Hey, man, it's OK," he said, backing into the waitress so that he was wedged between her and the man. Keeping his eyes on the Jamaican, Michael edged out from between them and away from the bar. "Hey, I was only asking her for our drinks, man. That's all." He raised his hands, palms out and inched toward their table. "I can wait," he said. "I'm just gonna sit down, now, and wait." He backed into his seat and looked toward Joanna and Dave.

The Jamaican yanked the knife from the bar top and tucked it into his belt. He pulled the waitress to him and whispered something into her ear. She laughed, nuzzling up to him, and called to the bartender, who reached into the cooler and set three Red Stripes on the counter.

Joanna rushed over to the table, followed by Dave.

"Jesus! That guy's out of his effing mind," Michael whispered to them.

"Are you okay?" Joanna asked.

Michael nodded.

"I know, man," Dave said. "Jamaicans can be really crazy about their women, really possessive, you know. You have to figure out who's with who and not get too close."

"But *she* was coming on to *me*," Michael said, glancing at Joanna.

The waitress came to stand at the table with their beers. "What Ah must get yuh to eat?" she said. She turned, looked around the room, then held her hand out to inspect her nails.

"Do you want to stay?" Joanna asked Michael.

He looked toward the bar where the Jamaican with the Yankees' cap stood with his back to their table. "I guess so. What do you think, Dave?"

Dave pushed back from the table and stretched his legs out in front of him. "I think it's okay. But I guess we better order something."

They ordered French fries and watched in silence until the waitress was out of earshot.

"Why are they so uptight around here?" Michael asked.

"Hey, this is a different culture, man," Dave said. "This is not the good old U.S. of A., you know." He laughed. "If you're going to mess around with the Jamaicans, you have to learn the rules. I've seen a lot of Americans get into trouble because they forgot they don't own the place."

"Like what?" Michael bit at a hangnail, his eyes darting around the room.

"Getting busted for drugs or trading money on the black market. Getting cut up over a woman. Hey, this is not some paradise." Dave gestured around the room and chuckled. "You just have to be careful. If you do the tourist thing and don't get too close to the Jamaicans, there's no real problem."

"But what about you? You live with Jamaicans," Michael

asked.

"Yeah, but Momma Samuel's different. She's older. She feels protective towards me. I moved in after this friend of mine left, so she sort of knew me. Besides," Dave hesitated, "the older Jamaicans have a certain respect for whites that the younger people don't. Maybe it comes from before independence." Dave bolted up and called across the room. "Hey, Jeevan!"

Their friend came swaggering towards them with his stars and stripes cap lowered jauntily over his brow. Pulling a chair from another table, Dave said, "Here, man, sit down. I'll buy you a beer."

Jeevan beamed at them with an impish smile through his missing front teeth. "I-ree. Peace, mahn." He had changed his clothes and wore a bright yellow shirt with large red flowers and a pair of chartreuse pants that fell about two inches above his sneaks. A cigarette dangled from his mouth, and the sweet smell of marijuana, like a mix of oregano and thyme, seemed to waft from his flesh. He smiled directly at Joanna and winked. She flushed and dropped her eyes. Jeevan turned to Michael, "Ah see yuh get some trouble, here, mahn. 'Im a rude boy, yuh know, for true, mahn." He shook his head. "Bomboclaat! 'Im like to mash up white boys." He leaned in close to Michael, wagging his head like an old woman dispensing wisdom. "Yuh must leave it, mahn."

"Leave what?" Michael asked, with a slight edge in his voice.

"Leave the woman, mahn. Leave the woman."

"What woman?" Michael looked at Joanna.

"No, mahn. De udder one," he said, jerking his head toward the waitress who was sitting at the bar.

"Jesus! All I did was ask her to get our drinks."

Jeevan flung back his head and cackled. "Dat good, mahn. Dat really good."

Michael looked at Joanna, then at Dave, and shrugged.

"Jeevan," Dave said. "Did you get the herb?"

Jeevan started. "Shhhh," he said, looking over his shoulder. "Bahkside, mahn! Not here. Yuh must come to me house tomorrow."

"How about us?" Michael asked.

"Yeh, mahn. Yuh must come wid 'im," Jeevan said. He looked across the table at Joanna. "Yuh come, too."

She turned to gaze at the dancers. "Maybe." She took Dave by the hand. "Let's dance."

CHAPTER SIX

Joanna awoke to the warmth of the sun creeping up her legs. She was damp with perspiration, and the sheets stuck to her skin. She dropped her legs over the side of the bed and sat up, squinting at the sun slanting through the green curtains. A slight breeze rippled through the window bringing with it the sounds of young girls' voices and rhythmic clapping. The children were playing a hand game just outside her window, and although they sang in patois, Joanna recognized the melody from her own childhood: "My boyfriend's name is Billy. He comes from dear old Philly."

She laughed and turned to look at the empty bed. Michael had risen early to meet Dave at Jeevan's. Later, she, Michael and Dave planned to drive inland to a small town about forty-five minutes from Negril. Michael wanted to call his business partner in the States, and the nearest phone was seventeen miles away at Savanna-la-Mar.

Michael had made a point of inviting Dave to go with them, and Joanna wondered if Michael just didn't want to be alone with her. The attraction she felt for Dave was growing stronger every day, but after all, Michael was her boyfriend, and she did love him. She touched the ring he had given her just a year ago. But, so far, this trip was not turning out like she had hoped.

She rested her elbows on the windowsill to watch the children outside. The girls were playing a new game now, chanting the same phrases over and over, dancing in a circle and pounding out the rhythm with their feet.

Joanna straightened up and stretched forward to touch her

toes. With her torso bent and her arms hanging limp in front of her, she swayed from side to side in rhythm to the girls' chant. "Sally when yuh marry, me wish yuh joy, firs' a gurl and t'en a boy ..."

She stood straight again and brought her arms up over her head, moving to the right, then the left, like a dancer limbering up. The pleasure of moving flooded her with sensations of dancing with Dave the night before. Dave was obviously attracted to her. So, she must still be a little bit desirable. But, why was Michael so distant? She went to stand before the small mirror over the bureau and stared at her reflection, hairbrush held in mid-air. Certainly, the first years of her relationship with Michael had been hard. They had been so young, and Joanna knew she had been very demanding of his attention. But she had never doubted that he loved her, even now she didn't really. But their life together had grown ... passionless. Even their love-making. That, too, had become more like a ritual, an obligation, rather than the burning merging it had once been. She sighed and walked to the shower stall, stripped out of her nightgown, and stepped in. With the water running, she didn't hear Michael come into the other room.

"We're back!" he called.

"Whoa, I'm not dressed." She grabbed a towel from the rack and wrapped it around herself, stepping out of the shower.

He stuck his head into the bathroom. "It's okay. It's just me. Dave and Jeevan are waiting on the porch."

"Dave and Jeevan?"

"Yeah, Jeevan's coming with us."

She wondered how many more people he was going to bring along. She pulled the towel from her body to dry her face and bent her head down to fluff her hair. "Hope you rented a car big enough for all of us."

Michael laughed. "Jeevan's got a friend who'll drive us for a couple dollars each."

"Sounds okay, I guess. Are you all ready to go?" She slid into her sandals.

"Yeah, we thought we'd just grab a couple of rolls on the way and eat when we get to Savanna-la-Mar." Michael fidgeted with the door handle.

"Fine. I'll be ready in a second."

He watched her as she rubbed the towel over her head. For a moment, she imagined she saw some of the old interest in his face, but then he said, "Have you noticed how attentive Dave is to you? I think he's into you."

She draped the towel around her body. "Doesn't that bother you?"

"No. Why should it?" He walked over to her and ran his finger down the bridge of her nose.

She pushed his hand away. "I don't know. Aren't you a little jealous?"

"I think it's flattering. I like it when other men think you're attractive." He glanced at his watch.

Joanna tilted her head up slightly so she could look him directly in the eye. "Don't you get jealous at all, ever?"

"Maybe a little, but I try not to. It's not like I own you or something. We're not married." He bent down and kissed her quickly on the cheek, his lips barely skimming her skin, and walked toward the door. "But I do love you. I'll wait for you on the porch," he said.

Joanna watched the door close, then hurled the towel at it. She finished dressing in a huff, threw some suntan oil and a wallet into her backpack, and went to join the men on the porch. Once outside, she raised her hand to shade her eyes from the glaring sun. Dave jumped to his feet and saluted, mimicking her gesture.

"Good morning, ma'am," he said, snapping to attention.

Joanna laughed and reached to lower his arm. Michael and Jeevan smirked at each other. Dave just grinned.

"Why are you guys grinning?" she asked. No one answered. "Oh, I see," she said, shifting her backpack to her shoulder. "You're all high, right?"

"Hey, we had to sample the product," Dave said while the other two continued to grin at her like dummies.

Another Jamaican man, biceps bulging through his fishnet t-shirt, lounged by a small beat-up car in the yard. She felt as if they were all waiting for a signal from her. She pulled her visor from her pack and put it on, then turned toward the men who were all staring, mesmerized. She thought they might start drooling any minute. "Boy, it must be good stuff. You guys are a bunch of zombies. Come on, let's go."

She bounded down the steps, and the men burst into motion, following her to the car. Jeevan got in the front with his friend Clive as Dave and Joanna slid into the cramped back seat.

"Small up yuhself. Dere little room in de bahk," Jeevan said.

Michael stood by the car rummaging in his pockets. "I can't find my lighter."

"You're just high," Joanna said and reached out the door to feel in his pocket. He slapped her hand away. "I've got it."

"I was just trying to help." She folded her arms across her chest and stared out the front window.

Michael held out his hand to show her the lighter, then got into the car. She refused to meet his eyes and shifted around to look to the window next to Dave. The car took off, a breeze blowing through the open window cooling her skin, hot with embarrassment.

At the center of town, they stopped by a roadside stand for something to eat. An elderly couple sat playing a game of dominoes under a small lean-to of poles and woven palm mats. They played on a metal table that shuddered and rang out each time the woman slammed down a tile. Around her head, she wore a narrow scarf tied in a band that sloped lopsided across her forehead, covering one eyebrow like a pirate's bandana. "Yuh play, mahn!" she shouted at the man.

He looked up, his eyes shooting open, took his red cap from his head, and scratched at his scalp. He considered the pieces on his palm, moving them around with his finger, as he eyed the dominos snaking across the table.

Joanna shoved into Michael so she could get out of the car. He went to lean against the hood. She nodded and smiled at the couple and inspected the food on the table. The woman waved her hand across the length of the table at the fruits and vegetables piled like tropical still-lifes. Several large platters held other foods under plastic covers. The woman reached for one to raise it. The aroma of sweet banana bread rose to Joanna's face like a wisp of perfumed chiffon as the woman lifted the cover. "Mmmm, smells good."

"Yuh buy some de nice pieces?" The woman smacked her lips.

"Just one minute, okay?" Joanna stuck her head in the car window. "You guys want some banana bread and fruit?"

"Sure, mahn," Dave said. The others nodded.

"How about you, Michael?"

"Huh? Yeah, sure. Whatever." He stared off, frowning into the distance as if he had more important things on his mind.

Joanna wondered what the hell was the matter with him. If he were any more distant, he'd be in another country. She swung back to the table and picked out some bananas and oranges while the woman wrapped the bread in a brown paper bag. Joanna handed the food to Jeevan through the window and gave the woman some money.

"Soon come bahk," the woman said and nudged the old man in his ribs. He looked up and smiled slowly, exposing a toothless grin, then waved his cap.

The car kicked up a steady trail of dust as they wound their way along the road, climbing into the jungle and leaving behind the gleaming sheet-of-turquoise-glass sea. They quickly finished their breakfast, and Joanna collected the remains in a bag, which she tucked under the seat.

"Well, it's definitely time for an after-breakfast joint," Dave said. "Whadda you think, Jeevan?"

"Sure, mahn. Is always time for good Jamaican herb. Ah roll a nice spleef for yuh, mahn." Jeevan pulled a plastic pouch stuffed with marijuana from his pants pocket and leaned back towards Joanna. "Where dat bag, mahn?" he asked.

She frowned. "What bag?"

"De paper bag, mahn. De paper bag." He pointed to her feet.

She bent forward to look under her seat. "It's filled with garbage." She pulled it out and wrinkled her nose.

"Bring it come," he said, gesturing for Joanna to give it to him.

"What for?" She held the dripping bag away from her lap.

"Fetch it, mahn. Fetch it." Jeevan seemed about ready to jump over the seat.

"He wants the bag," Michael said.

"I don't need an interpreter," she snapped.

One side of the bag dripped where it had been lying on the floor. Jeevan grabbed it and started throwing orange rinds and banana peels out the window. He ripped the bag and threw the wet parts out until he had a piece of dry paper about six inches square. He pulled the marijuana, like strands of matted hair, from his pouch and placed them in the center of the paper, rolling a joint the size of a cone-shaped cigar.

"Good spleef, mahn," he said, puffing while Dave held a lighter to the end.

They passed the joint around. Joanna drew deeply each time it came to her, wanting to lose herself in the drug's warm, fuzzy comfort, and soon she was aware of little except the sensations of her body. Her thighs pressed against Michael on one side and Dave on the other in the cramped, sweltering car. She thought of moving her leg away from Dave's; it was the polite thing to do. But she liked the feel of his hairs like a furry log tickling her skin. On the other side, Michael's leg felt smooth and sticky. Gradually, all her attention began to focus on where her leg touched Michael's, and her desire to move away grew like a twitching sensation, rising from the point where they touched, through her whole body up to her throat until she felt like she might scream. For a second, it seemed to Joanna as if the rest of her life might depend on whether or not she moved her leg. Suddenly, the car lurched, throwing them to one side as Clive swerved to avoid a car heading into their lane.

"Crazy Jamaican drivers," Dave muttered under his breath, leaning to grab the front seat as the car passed without hitting them.

Michael pulled his leg away from Joanna's. "Sticky, isn't it?" he said, running his hand along the side of his leg. She nodded. Dave's thigh was still pressed firmly against hers despite the swerve of the car. She rested her head on the back of her seat, sinking into a sweaty, marijuana haze.

The car began to descend, and soon a few houses appeared out of the mass of palm trees and shrubbery that bordered the road. As they neared Savanna-la-Mar, the road flattened out, and they drove into town on the long, dusty main street, teeming with people. Clive stopped the car in front of what looked like a courthouse, a two-story, white building with pillars spaced along its front. On the sidewalk in front of the courthouse stood a solitary phone, under a metal canopy and open to the street.

Jeevan and Clive conferred in patois, then Jeevan said, "Dis de phone, mahn. Yuh must use it here."

"This is the phone?" Michael said. "I mean, isn't there one inside somewhere?"

"Dis de phone, mahn. It work good," said Jeevan. He nodded toward Clive. "'Im must leave de car here. We soon come bahk."

"Why don't we all meet back here in two hours?" Dave said.

They agreed. The three Americans watched as Jeevan and Clive strolled away.

When they were alone, Michael said, "Boy, is this primitive. Do you have any change?"

Joanna rummaged in the bottom of her bag and pulled out several coins. She and Dave drifted over to lean on the hood of the car while Michael made his call.

Joanna took in the scene around her. The street was full of Jamaicans rambling by as if they had nowhere in particular to go and no particular time to be there. They paraded past in clothes of every conceivable color: day-glow pinks, yellows, chartreuses, reds, purples, patterns and colors jarring and clashing in wild combinations. She reached into her bag for her sunglasses and slipped them on as if to protect her eyes from the bright colors.

Dave watched her, smiling. "Now you really look like a tourist."

She laughed. "Right. I needed the sunglasses. My sun-burned skin wasn't enough." Even with her sunglasses on, the bright sun glared fiercely. She pulled her visor lower to shade her eyes. Dave swung around to the other side so the sun was behind her.

"Is that better?" he asked.

Joanna nodded. "Thanks. That was sweet of you."

Dave took a little bow. "Just trying to be a gentleman, my lady. Hey, listen, I know a funky little restaurant where we can get some great ackee and rice. Then we can hit the market."

"Yeah, I've had it. It's good. Sort of like spicy scrambled eggs, right?"

"For true, mahn. It's the national dish." Dave looked past Joanna, raised his chin, and gestured to something behind her. Joanna turned to see Michael striding toward them, frowning.

"This is screwed up," Michael said. "I have to wait here until a line to the mainland opens up. The operator said it could be half an hour to forty-five minutes."

"Yeah, that happens a lot," Dave said.

"Can you try later?" Joanna asked.

"She said she'd call back when a line opens. But if I leave, I lose my turn, and then I'd just have to wait again later." He kicked at a scrap of paper on the sidewalk. "There's no reason for you two to hang around. Why don't you and Dave go walk around and meet me back here in an hour."

"Don't you want company? I'll stay if you want," Joanna said. She checked the large clock atop the courthouse steeple.

"No, that's okay, Jo. You go with Dave."

"Yeah, come on," Dave said, taking her arm. "Let's go get some ackee."

Joanna shrugged. She turned back to ask Michael if they should bring him something to eat, but he was already half-way across the broad street, heading for a small shop.

"Come on. He's okay," Dave said, his hand on Joanna's elbow. He led her along the main street toward the center of town. In the market, the shops and sidewalks were a jumble of color, like the Jamaicans themselves who milled around the street. Joanna browsed through clothing strung on ropes hung across the sidewalk, ducking under to get from one row to another. More clothes were stacked high on tables and piled on chairs at shops along the way.

Dave pulled out a skimpy little blouse from a pile. "Hey, this would look good on you," he said.

Joanna took the piece from him and held it up to her chest. "Might be a little too risqué for me," she said and laid it back down. "Let's look at that shop over there."

They inched their way through the tangle of shoppers. The strong smells of bodies sweaty from work under a hot sun, engulfed her as she and Dave moved through the throng. Horns blew, bells clanged, children hooted, bombarding her ears as well. It was bedlam.

Dave pulled her into a little side street where the confusion subsided somewhat. He steered her into a store-front restaurant in the middle of the block. Alone in the restaurant, they chose a table against the wall.

"Whew!" Joanna said, collapsing into a chair. "That was a madhouse."

"Yeah, it's wild." He pulled out the seat across from her and sat down.

She set her visor next to her and sighed. "Well, we certainly seem to be spending a lot of time together, don't we?"

"Fine with me," Dave said and settled comfortably into his chair.

The kitchen door swung open and the waitress, a heavy woman, came waddling towards them. Dave ordered two Red Stripes and some ackee, salt fish, and rice for them both while Joanna stared at the table and played with the tableware.

When they were alone again, she said, "Michael doesn't seem to be uptight about us at all."

Dave hunched forward and seemed to consider his words. "Hard to say. But not very much. Does that bother you?"

"A little." Joanna looked out the large window at the front of the restaurant. A man led a parade of small goats on a long tether past the window.

Dave followed her gaze. "He probably just has other things on his mind." He turned toward her and picked up the spoon Joanna was fingering. "Hey, you like me, right?"

She smiled and nodded.

"And I like you. So, let's just enjoy each other's company, okay?"

She laughed and glanced back toward the kitchen where the waitress was preparing their order. The heavy woman lumbered over with beers in one hand and two platters balanced on her forearm. Each plate was heaped high with a bulbous yellow substance mixed with rice and fish. Bright pieces of red pepper made a colorful accent to the yellow ackee. Joanna tasted her food and began fanning her face. "Whoa," she said, grabbing for her beer. "Hot!"

"Sure, mahn," Dave said. "The hot make you sweat. Keep you cool in the heat, mahn." They laughed as Joanna wiped tears from her eyes.

"How'd you ever find this place?" She took another tentative mouthful.

"Hey, mahn, I've been around," Dave said.

"I bet you have."

They finished lunch and ventured back onto the main street. A half-dozen older women knelt on their haunches by the curb to sell fresh fish wrapped in newspapers and brown paper. Their brightly flowered dresses dazzled like a wild, day-glow garden in bloom. Scattered among the other stands, food vendors sold spicy meat patties or sweet cakes from carts that looked as if they might need a good scrubbing. Kids scampered everywhere, running in between and under the stands, playing tag around the fish women who scolded them in patois. Goats and pigs ran loose in the street, venturing onto the sidewalk for some juicy morsel dropped by chance, or rummaging through the piles of garbage that grew around each stand.

"Yuk." Joanna eyed the stout pigs and edged closer to Dave. "I hope they don't get too close to me."

"I'll protect you," he said and laughed.

Packed everywhere between the stands were people, hustling and jostling each other, haggling and making off with their goods in slow motion to the reggae music that flowed from dozens of transistor radios. Out on the street, a group of men lounged beside some motorcycles, their muscled arms folded across their chests, the Jamaican version of Hell's Angels, Joanna thought. As they strolled by, someone called out.

"Hey, Joanna, yuh lookin' fine!"

She turned, surprised. Jeevan detached himself from the crowd and walked toward her and Dave.

"Yuh appreciatin' de Jamaican scenery, sistah?" he asked.

"Sort of overwhelming," Joanna said, laughing.

"You get used to it," Dave said.

Jeevan clasped Dave's hand firmly and said, "Broddah, how yuh be, mahn?" as if they hadn't seen each other in days. They raised their hands shoulder-high and high-fived.

"I'm great, brother," Dave said. "What's happening?"

"Ah just visitin' wid my broddahs, here. Is man's talk we makin' to pass de time."

He turned toward Joanna. "Ah tellin' my broddahs, yuh fine 'Merican lady," he said. "Where yuh mahn? Doan he getting' mad 'cause yuh wid dis udder mahn Dave?"

Joanna chuckled as if Jeevan's question were ridiculous. "No, he's not mad," she said. "He thinks it's great for me to have men friends."

Jeevan gave a long, low whistle. "Really, mahn? 'Im some crazy fuckah."

"Yeah," she said, a half-smile playing on her lips.

Jeevan looked from Joanna to Dave and smirked. "Well, mahn. Ah must go talk business wid my broddahs. Ah see yuh likkle more den. I-ree, mahn."

"He's in a friendly mood," Joanna said as Jeevan walked away.

"He's just showing off his American friends to his buddies."

CHAPTER SEVEN

They ambled through the market again until they came to a little side street. Dave said he knew a nice bar where they could get another beer before they met Michael. They walked down cement steps into a cramped, dark basement below a record store. The place was deserted except for the bartender, a short Jamaican with darting eyes. Dave got two beers and sat next to Joanna in one of the booths.

"Joanna, what's going on between you and Michael? Are you guys having trouble?"

"I'm not sure. But, I really don't want to talk about it. It's too depressing."

He reached for her hand. "You know, I don't want to interfere, but I think Michael would be really stupid to do anything to lose you."

Joanna smiled, holding back tears. "Thanks."

"I mean it." He put his finger under her chin and lifted her face to lean in for a kiss.

She pulled back slowly. "Dave, no. I'm too confused."

"I know you are," he said, running his finger lightly across her cheek. "There's no hurry. You and Michael try to work it out. I'm here if you need to talk."

They finished their beers in silence and headed to the courthouse. Michael was sitting on the car hood reading a magazine. He jumped off and walked toward them. "Hi. Did you guys have a good time?"

Joanna reddened and glanced at Dave. "It was fun," she said. "Did you get through to the office?"

"Yeah, I did." He bit his lip.

"What's the matter?" Joanna reached out and touched his arm. A bus brimming with people rushed by them so close that Joanna caught a whiff of the chickens on board. Michael yanked her out of the way.

"Hey, watch out," Dave yelled at the receding bus. "God, they're crazy in town. Let's get out of the street."

When they were back by the car, Joanna asked again, "Michael, what's the matter?"

"Well, nothing really. In fact, it's good." But he wasn't smiling.

"Then why the long face?" she asked.

Michael jiggled some coins in his pocket and nodded toward Dave, who took the magazine from Michael and went to sit on the curb out of earshot.

"So, what happened?" Joanna said.

"Well, we got that big job I told you about." Michael glanced behind him like someone might be listening. He ran his hand over his mouth.

Joanna narrowed her eyes and looked at him over the top of her sunglasses. "So?"

He inspected his sandals, then looked up at Joanna. "Listen, Jo, I have to go back. Ted can't handle it alone."

"Go back! What the hell are you talking about?" Joanna ripped her sunglasses off and stared at him. "We've only been here a week. We've got another three to go."

Michael sighed. "I know, but I have to go back."

Joanna swung around to face him. "I thought this was supposed to be our big vacation. Who's been telling me to relax since we got here? I thought you said Ted could handle everything himself."

"Well, he could have, but they moved the delivery date up."

"Great. That's great." Joanna paced in front of him. "Go ahead. Ruin our damn vacation because they decided to move the fucking date up. What about me? What about us?"

"Jo, be reasonable. I have to go back." He grabbed her arm to stop her pacing. "Calm down."

"Stop telling me to calm down, for God's sake. I'm so sick of hearing you say that." She wrenched her arm from his grip.

"Listen, you don't have to go if you'd rather stay here. I wouldn't mind. There's no reason to ruin your vacation just because I have to work. Why don't you think about staying?"

Joanna's eyes shot open. "Stay here! Why would I stay here alone?"

He dropped his hand and shrugged. "Why not? You can take care of yourself. And besides, you don't have to stay by yourself. You could probably rent a room from Dave. He's got two bedrooms, doesn't he?"

Joanna stared at him as bile rose in her throat. "You want me to stay with Dave?" She could barely keep from screaming the words.

"Why not?" he answered. "I trust you."

"You trust me! Of course, you trust me. But why should I trust you? For all I know, you're having a god-damn affair, and that's why you're going back. Is that it? Is that why you have to go back?"

"Jo, it's not like that at all."

Suddenly her body went slack, all the strength drained from her every muscle. She felt bone-tired. "What about wanting to be together?" she asked. "What about that?"

"Jo, we don't have to spend every single moment of our lives together."

"I know. Michael, you really don't have to tell me again."

Michael reached for her hand. "There's no reason why you have to leave here if you don't want to. There's time to think about it, anyway. I'll be here another four days. Why don't you think about it?"

"You already changed your flight? You bastard. I can't believe it." She yanked her arms back and raised her hands to ward off his touch. "Get away from me. Oh, I'll think about it all right," she said and strode around the car to Dave.

***

By the time they reached Negril, it was late afternoon. Clive and Jeevan dropped Joanna and the men off in front of High Hat's and drove away in a cloud of dust and sand. One by one, Joanna, then Michael and Dave drifted over to the steps and sat down to stare out at the sea. The sun glimmered across the water in a straight line like a finger pointed at Joanna's heart. She knew she would have to decide. But how could she?

A woman walked by on the road, one hand balancing a basket brimming with clothes on her head, the other clinging to the hand of a young child who toddled by her side. The woman's feet were hidden by the advancing dusk, and she appeared to glide with the slow, majestic grace of a queen on a litter, her feet never touching the ground, the child trailing silently next to her like a tiny attendant.

When they had passed, Dave leaned back against the banister to face Joanna. "It's really a drag that you guys have to leave early. We were having a great time," he said.

Neither Joanna nor Michael answered. The quiet felt like a hushed courtroom before the verdict. Even the jukebox was mute. Only the soft swishing of sea on sand murmured, breaking the strained silence.

Joanna spoke up. "I was thinking maybe I'd stay when Michael leaves." It was more a question than anything else.

Dave looked puzzled. Michael sat stone-faced.

When she didn't go on, Michael recovered and picked up the cue. "Actually, there's no reason for her to come back with me right now. We were going to stay another three weeks, anyway, and when I get back, I'll be really busy on this catalog, working nights late, probably weekends." He leaned forward and straightened her shoulder strap. "I think it makes more sense for you to stay and enjoy yourself as long as you're here. It'll be good for you."

Joanna and Michael both turned to look at Dave. The dusk was falling quickly, and their faces were already in the shadows. Dave rubbed his hands over his bare knees and coughed. "Hey, why not," he said.

Joanna's throat tightened. She swallowed hard and forced the words out. "Michael and I were talking about whether it was cool for me to stay by myself," she said. She looked toward Michael, who seemed to nod ever so slightly in the dim light.

"Well, it's not that great an idea for you to stay alone," Dave said.

A slight breeze rippled over Joanna, making her shiver. She wanted another shirt but didn't dare break the mood by getting up. She felt as if the three of them were deciding her fate.

Michael said, "I thought maybe it would make sense for her to rent your extra room." His words dropped like stones into the approaching darkness.

Dave cleared his throat. "Uh, yeah, I got plenty of room. I guess that would be okay." He leaned forward and hunched over his legs. "I mean, it really isn't that smart for an American woman to be down here alone."

Michael jumped up, startling Joanna and Dave. "Listen, you two," he said. "This is crazy. Why are we pretending? We're grown-ups, right?"

Joanna and Dave stared at him.

"Let's be mature about this. I know you don't want to go home, Jo, and I know you guys really like each other. So why don't we all just admit what's happening? I mean, you can do what you want while you're here; it's okay with me. We've talked about this, Jo, and now's as good a time as any to try it. I'll do my thing. You'll do yours, and we'll call it a vacation. Does that make sense?"

Dave made a move to stand up. "Maybe you two should discuss this alone," he said.

Michael put his hand on Dave's arm. "Hey, man, it's okay. We've talked about an open relationship before, haven't we, Jo?"

She bolted up and stomped away from the men, then swung around to face them in the dark. "Michael, you could be a little more subtle. I'm not sure I'm ready for true confessions. And talking about it and doing it are two different things."

"I really think you guys need to talk about this alone," Dave said.

"No, no, it's okay. We can work it out. Can't we, Jo?" Michael said. He reached over and rested both hands on Dave's shoulder. "Hey, I like you, man. Otherwise, I couldn't feel good about this."

"That's real nice. But I'm not really into breaking up any relationships, you know. I'm more into just going with the flow."

"Oh, come on, Dave!" Michael's voice took on a sharp edge. "That hasn't kept you from coming on to her before now."

"Michael!" Joanna stepped between the men and took Michael's arm. "Hey, I'm right here, remember? And that's not fair!"

"Why not? It's true," he said, sounding like a petulant child.

"Well, so what?" Joanna snapped, "You didn't seem to mind."

"Hey, listen, man," Dave said, "I'm really not into this. First, you tell Joanna to move in with me, then you get pissed because I like her. Which is it?"

By now it was too dim to see anything but the outline of Michael's form. The night insects had taken up their evening clatter, and it sounded to Joanna like the clicking of a thousand tongues.

Finally, Michael answered. "You're right. It does bother me—what's going on between you two—but I know it shouldn't. I mean, I know this might be crazy, but I have been feeling a little jealous ..."

"Jealous!" Joanna blurted out. "Well, you certainly don't act it."

"Well, yeah, I've been trying to keep it together. I mean, you've got a right to do whatever you want, and so do you, man," he said, turning to Dave. "I don't see a relationship as some kind of prison."

Joanna sat down on the steps, ran her fingers through her hair, and gazed into the distance. A reggae song wailed from the bar. She had a fleeting image of herself auctioned off, Dave and Michael with hands raised to call their bids. "This is too crazy," she said. Then turning to Dave, "But, I would feel a lot safer staying with you, Dave, if I do decide to stay."

Dave picked up his shirt from the step and pulled it over his head. "Michael, are you sure this is what you want? Suppose Jo decides she wants to stay here longer? How are you going to feel?"

"I have to take that chance."

"Take that chance? What do you mean?" Joanna asked.

It was too dark to see Michael's face, to pick up any clues from his expression, but she could tell from his stance, from the way he hung his head down, that he didn't want to answer. It was so annoying, really, to be able to read him so well that she knew before he spoke what he was feeling. So infuriating to know before he said it that she would be unhappy about whatever he would answer. Still, she had to know. "Why do you have to take that chance, Michael?" she asked, again.

"Okay. Listen." He stopped and looked at Joanna. "Because if I want the same freedom for myself, I have to give it to you."

She watched him, staring at his dark frame, her eyes wide, her mouth slightly open, poised to ask another question, hoping to get a different answer. She had known his answer would hurt, and it had. "I see," she said. She got up and walked across the sandy yard toward the road. The porch lights came on, drawing her eyes back to the men, who were both watching her in the glare of the light. She turned away and stood by the fence listening to the sea now that the music had stopped for a moment. The water stretched out into the night, immense, without form, without end, its waves muttering darkly. So, he wanted his freedom. She wasn't really sure she wanted hers, or was she just too scared to admit it? Still, there was Dave. The music began again. She turned quickly and walked back to the men. "I'm staying," she said. "Can I stay with you, Dave?"

"Fine with me. Any time."

"Good. I'll move in after Michael leaves in a few days. Let me know how much you want for rent. That's that, then." She moved toward the door. "I'm going in to take a shower. Are you coming, Michael?"

Michael and Dave looked at each other. Then Michael shrugged and jumped up. "See you later, Dave," he said and hurried after Joanna.

***

Once inside, a prickly nervousness seemed to descend over them, driving them out towards the night, like mosquitoes fleeing the scent of citronella in the room. They hurriedly changed their clothes and decided to walk down to Chicken Little, a small restaurant close by, for some dinner. As they strolled along the road, with only the gentle sounds of the sea for company, Michael took Joanna's hand. His touch warmed her hand and her heart.

"It'll be okay," he said. "We should try it."

"If you say so, Michael. But it scares me. I'm not really sure I'm into this open relationship stuff. In theory, it's one thing, but in practice? I'm not sure."

He put his arm around her shoulders, and a longing for him and the times they had shared together washed over Joanna, dampening her anger and pain. She so wanted to feel again like she had when things were still good between them. They came to a section of the road where a path led down to the water. The stars in the night sky seemed to twinkle in rhythm with the surf. Joanna took her sandals off, and Michael did, too. She took his hand again and led him down to the water where they stood gazing up at the sky.

"It's beautiful, isn't it," she said.

"Yeah, this is what vacations are all about."

"Remember the first time we came to Jamaica?" She hugged him around his waist. Despite it all, she still wanted to have him close. They had had so many good times together.

"Hmmm. We had just gotten back together. That was a hard six months."

They had been separated briefly about five years ago. When the anger and hurt had subsided somewhat, they had begun seeing each other again. Soon they were spending all their time together. Shortly after, they spent a week in Jamaica.

"We were inseparable that trip," Joanna said.

Michael sighed. "I know. It's as if we need to be separated in order to appreciate each other. Why is that?"

"Oh, Michael, I wish I knew." She turned and laid her head against his chest. "But, I wish it wasn't that way.

He held her tightly. "Maybe when you come home, and we've had a little space, things will be really good again."

"Michael, I don't really want a little space. Suppose we end up splitting up?"

He stroked her hair as they stood quietly together. Wrapped in Michael's arms, Joanna felt secure again like a tiny star snuggled in the velvety Jamaican sky. She just wished she could forget everything else but how it had once been between them.

"Sometimes I think you do want space, and you just don't know it," he said. As he spoke, a wave caught them where they stood and swirled around their ankles. As the water receded, it left a depression around their feet.

"I'm sinking," Joanna said, pulling her feet from the sucking sand. "Do you think that means something?" She laughed, but the sound was closer to a cry. "I know absence is supposed to make the heart grow fonder, but what about out of sight, out of mind? Suppose I decide I like my freedom, too?'

"Oh, Jo, don't worry so much," Michael said, pulling her from the water's edge. "A little time apart will be good for us."

She walked ahead of him toward the road. "I hope so, but I'm not so sure. This on and off again is beginning to wear a little thin."

CHAPTER EIGHT

T he day of the baptism, Joanna put a skirt on for the first time since coming to Jamaica. She grabbed a tank top to go with it, sure that the heat would be unbearable in the church. Yet, she felt excited to see a side of Jamaica that most tourists never would. She watched Michael button his shirt collar. "You look pretty snazzy," she said. "Must be going to a funeral."

He laughed. "I feel like I am. I'm just glad I'll be taking pictures, so I won't have to pray."

Joanna sat on the bed, pulling on her sandals. "Actually, it could be pretty interesting. Do you think maybe people'll start to speak in tongues?"

"You think they might? I could get some great shots."

Joanna smiled. "Maybe."

Michael packed up his cameras while Joanna finished putting on her mascara. They left for Jeevan's, walking slowly under the sweltering sun. Jeevan, Dahlia, and Christopher sat waiting in front of the house, looking for all the world like a Caribbean version of a mid-western American family in their Sunday best. Jeevan seemed more mature but out of sorts without his stars and stripes wool cap. But Dahlia beamed in a dark green dress with puffy sleeves, transformed into a respectable matron despite plump knees showing beneath her short skirt. The baby sat on her lap, decked out in a gold-colored outfit with matching shorts and bib.

Joanna tickled the baby under his arms. He giggled and turned to hide his face in his mother's chest.

"Today, yuh be baptized, Christopher," Dahlia said to him. He smiled and reached to put his arms around her neck.

"Does he have a middle name?" Joanna asked.

Jeevan answered in a low voice, "We namin' 'im Lee in de church." He pulled a spliff from his shirt pocket, offering it to Joanna and Michael. "We smoke dis before we go." He held the spliff high and laughed. "We must celebrate 'im name day." Without waiting for an answer, he stepped into the house.

Michael followed, turning in the doorframe to Joanna. "Are you coming?"

She shook her head. "It doesn't seem right to get high before we go to a church."

Michael shrugged and followed Jeevan.

Joanna reached for the baby, who held his sweetly chubby arms out to her. She took him from Dahlia and sat down on one of the chairs that leaned up against the house, bouncing him on her knees. She clapped his pudgy hands between hers and began to sing the words to a popular song, "Christopher Lee, sing it to me, Christopher Lee, sing it to me."

Suddenly, Dahlia leaned forward to snatch the baby away, a look of horror on her face as if Joanna were a demon attacking her baby. Christopher began to cry, frightened by his mother's quick movements.

"Dahlia, what's the matter?"

"Yuh curse 'im on 'im name day," the woman answered, the words themselves sounding like a curse.

"I was just singing to him," "Joanna said.

"Yuh give 'im name away outside de church. Udder people hear and work a curse on 'im." Now it was Joanna's turn to stare in horror. "Ah tellin' yuh, yuh say both 'im name." Dahlia hugged the baby close to her and turned to her side as if to shield Christopher from Joanna.

"His full name? What's the matter with that?" Joanna felt a chill run down her back and shivered.

"In Jamaica, dat a t'ing full of danger." Dahlia rocked Christopher back and forth, trying to calm his crying. She jutted her chin out and refused to look at Joanna.

Joanna reached over and touched Dahlia's arm. "I'm so sorry. I didn't realize." She leaned forward to look directly into Dahlia's eyes, trying hard to communicate with her heart where words were failing. "We don't think like that in my country."

Dahlia huffed as she continued rocking the baby and looked away again.

Jeevan came to the door and reached over Dahlia to give the baby a shake. "Why 'im makin' such a mess of noise? 'Im must quit dis fuss on 'im name day."

"Dahlia is upset because I said Christopher's full name out loud," Joanna said.

Jeevan nodded with the solemnity of a judge. "Jamaican custom, mahn. Maybe true, maybe no."

Joanna's rational mind told her that Dahlia's fears were silly superstitions, but something nagging inside her wasn't so sure. She had heard enough about voodoo and black magic to know the power of suggestion could kill. She turned to look at the bushes by the side of the house. The inviting, lush greenery had become a threatening jungle. Should she search there to make sure no one had been close enough to hear her singing? A deep sense of dread settled on her, weighing her down, making it hard to breathe. Suppose something did happen to the baby? How would she feel then?

Jeevan jumped down from the house. "Doan worry wid dat, sistah," he said, "Is time to go."

"Where's Dave?" Joanna asked. "Wasn't he supposed to meet us here?"

"Yeh, mahn," said Jeevan, "but it too late. We must leave widout dat mahn. Come, now."

They picked up their things and headed down the road, Joanna walking with the men, Dahlia leading in front with the baby.

***

The Jamaican First Baptist Church sat in the middle of a lush green lawn about three-quarters of a mile down the road on the way out of town. Grass was a rare sight in Negril and represented a hard-won victory over the wildness of the bush by the church deacon. The white stucco building looked palatial in comparison to the shacks of the Jamaicans, and slightly out of place.

A small crowd milled in front of the door, mostly women. Dahlia wandered over to the women, who clustered around her to coo at Christopher. She smiled proudly as she held her son, clearly delighted to be the center of attention. Joanna, Michael, and Jeevan waited apart from the group while Michael loaded his camera.

Dahlia called out, "Michael. Come now. Yuh must come take de pikcha wid me friends."

The women lined up in a straight row with Dahlia and the baby in the center. Joanna was struck by how stiff and uncomfortable the Jamaicans looked as they posed in their church finery. Gone were the vibrant colors of the market in Savanna-la-Mar. Instead, the women wore light-colored dresses with their arms modestly covered. The only bright colors were on their hats adorned with sprigs of artificial flowers. One woman wore white Mary Janes, polished to a gleaming shine, too big for her delicate frame, but which gave her a sweet air of youthful innocence. None of them smiled for the photo as if the occasion were too solemn for any show of gaiety.

Joanna felt suddenly out of place in her tank top and skirt, as if she too should be covered up. Dahlia's reaction to her song had set Joanna on edge. Her delight that destiny had somehow led her to this baptism had evaporated, replaced by a vague sense of menace. Now, she stood sweating in the hot sun and hoped that the baptism ceremony would be brief. She longed to be free of her clinging clothes and the suffocating cloud that hung over her.

The church bell struck, calling the worshippers inside. As they walked toward the chapel, Jeevan turned to Joanna. "Yuh must sit wid Dahlia. Make big honor for 'im and me."

The prospect didn't thrill Joanna, but she nodded and hurried ahead to join Dahlia. The church was tiny with only a few double pews filling the space. Several prints of Bible scenes decorated the walls, and a large crucifix hung at the front of the church. Joanna followed Dahlia into the second pew, avoiding eye contact with her. Michael waited at the back of the church, his camera ready, Jeevan with him, and Joanna had a moment of panic at being alone with Dahlia. She forced herself to smile at the woman and the baby.

The preacher stood behind the wooden pulpit, a large, corpulent man dressed in a black suit and a starched white shirt, both stretched to bursting by his bulk. His high collar pressed so tightly against his neck that a roll of flesh hung over it. To his right, three solemn women waited, dressed in prim white blouses with flared sleeves and wearing black skirts well below their knees. Their tasseled mortarboard hats reminded Joanna of a high school graduation but lent the women an air of dignity. Next to the women, a teenage boy, holding a guitar, perched on a stool. At a signal from the preacher, he began strumming, and the women joined in the song, holding their hymnals before them and swaying in unison to the music. The congregation joined them, and soon the small church rocked with voices.

After the hymns, the preacher called Dahlia to the back of the church with Christopher. He took the baby and, holding him by his back and feet, dipped the top of his head into a small basin on a pedestal. The baby didn't make a sound but sucked contentedly on his fingers during the dunking. Dahlia beamed.

With the baptism completed, the preacher launched into his sermon. Speaking quietly, he exhorted his followers to good deeds. But soon, caught up in his own message, his voice boomed louder and louder as he recounted the evils of sin.

"And the wages of sin are damnation!"

"Amen," called a few voices.

"The evil doers among you shall surely burn in hell. And the reward of sinners will be eternal suffering, and hear me now, they will never behold the face of our Lord, Jesus Christ."

"Yes, Jesus. Yes, for true." Now voices began to swell all around Joanna.

"So therefore, I beseech you to follow the Lord's commandments or surely you will be damned for all time."

The whole congregation responded in many voices, "Amen. Amen, Lord."

"And harken unto me, for surely, I have heard the voice of God, and he has commanded me to say to you, 'How many of you have followed the path of righteousness, for surely, you and you alone will be delivered from the fires of hell.'"

Voices all around Joanna rang out. "Ah 'ave. Ah 'ave. Ah heard de Lord's voice. Ah follow de path."

"Then let us rise and sing praises to His name."

On cue, the young man struck his guitar, and the three women broke into a lively spiritual. The congregation took up the chorus, chanting it over and over. Most of the women swayed to the music. A young girl in the front pew, her blue pill box hat falling over her eyes, jumped in place as an older woman fanned her. Dahlia sat Christopher on the pew next to her and began clapping and rocking to the music. The tempo of the hymn picked up with people all around Joanna joining in the jubilation. Voices cried out from behind her, "Ah hear yuh, Lord. Yes, yes. Lord, I believe. Jesus, I believe."

Joanna felt dizzy with the heat and the noise. She heard a loud thump to her side and turned to see a plump, middle-aged woman on the floor. She lay moaning, her floral dress gathered around her thighs, revealing her thrashing legs. No one else seemed to notice. Joanna turned toward the front in time to see the young girl with the blue hat collapse onto the pew, twitching violently. Joanna looked behind her for Michael. He was running up and down the aisles snapping shots as fast as he could. Jeevan, standing near the door, caught her eye and winked. Joanna began to edge past Dahlia. She was desperate to get outside, away from the sweating bodies, the shouting, the heat—she couldn't breathe. Suddenly, Dahlia grabbed Joanna's arms and began shaking her. The woman's face was so close to Joanna's that their noses were almost touching, and Joanna was awash in Dahlia's hot breath.

"Sinner, sinner," she shouted at Joanna. "Yuh sinner, repent, repent, before it too late!"

Joanna wrenched herself from the bigger woman's grasp and stumbled into the aisle. Jumping over the woman still shuddering on the floor, she ran for the door. Once outside, she hunched over, hands on her knees, gasping fresh air. She looked up to see Michael standing beside her.

"What's wrong?" he asked.

"What's wrong? They're crazy in there," she said. "Dahlia started shaking me and calling me a sinner. She thinks I put some kind of a curse on the baby. That's what the hassle was about back at the house. She totally freaked me out."

Michael squatted and rested his camera bag on the ground, intent on arranging the equipment in the bag. "Don't worry about it. She probably got carried away with the singing and all those people rolling around, that's all. Probably didn't even know what she was doing."

"I don't know, Michael. You should have seen her eyes."

***

They were dressing for breakfast the next morning when they heard a knock on the door. Joanna cocked her head and glanced at Michael, who was zipping up his pants. He frowned and shrugged. She hurriedly pulled her top down over her chest.

"Who is it?" she called.

"It's Dave."

Michael squinted and scowled as she went to open the door.

"Sorry to barge in on you," Dave said, pulling a piece of paper from his pocket. He looked ashen under his tan, dark circles under his eyes, his pupils black pits. "I just got this." His hand shook as he passed the slip to Joanna.

It was a telegram: "COME IMMEDIATELY STOP DAD HAVING

BRAIN SURGERY STOP MOTHER."

Joanna handed Michael the telegram. "What's it mean?" she asked Dave.

"Not sure." He shook his head and ran his hands through his hair. "I just talked to them a couple of weeks ago, and everything was fine. Now I get this." He took the paper from Michael and folded it back in his pocket.

"Brain surgery sounds sorta serious," Michael said.

Dave blanched. "I wished she had said more. But, whatever, I have to go." He turned to Joanna. "Listen, I don't know when I'll be back. It all depends on what happens at home. I'm going to Montego Bay today to get a flight out." He moved closer to Joanna. "I'm really sorry about this. It's crazy. If I know my mother, he's probably having a mole removed from his forehead." He forced a laugh and went on, talking fast as if trying to get everything in before Joanna could speak. "You can still stay at my place. Don't worry about the rent. It's paid for a month. Who knows? Maybe I'll be back in a week. Momma Samuel will take good care of you. She wouldn't even think of cheating you or anything. And she's a great cook." He fell silent and shifted from foot to foot like an embarrassed little kid.

The three of them stood staring at each other. Then Dave stepped forward and shook Michael's hand. He turned back to Joanna, who blinked to keep from crying. He put his hands on her shoulders. "I'm really, really sorry it worked out this way."

She nodded, her arms limp at her sides like a ragdoll. "There's nothing you can do about it. I understand." She gave him a half-smile. "Do whatever you have to do, Dave. Don't worry about me. Your father's the most important thing now."

He leaned forward and hugged her awkwardly. Then turned to wave at Michael. "See you," he said and disappeared through the door.

When he had gone, Joanna slumped onto the bed, staring vacantly. "What a drag about his father. So sudden. Hope he'll be okay."

Michael sat down beside her and took her hand. "Yeah, it's a bummer. But you know, it's fine if you want to come home with me."

She ran her finger along the veins on the back of his hand. "It's weird, isn't it? You're leaving. Now he's leaving. Everybody's leaving me." She managed a slight laugh. "I don't know, Michael. I feel like I should still stay. Sort of like it was supposed to happen like this, like I was supposed to stay here alone." She hesitated, worried that he would say what she was thinking was just her being silly. She turned to look at him. "You know that night when we went to the Paradise, after Jeevan's?" Michael, nodded. "Well, I was high, of course, and I had this vision or warning or something, I don't know what to call it. But it looked like you and Dave just disappeared, like you were plucked away by some invisible hand. And that's what this is like. Like you've both been plucked away."

"Oh, Jo. That's crazy. It's just coincidence. I thought maybe you were getting over all that crap. You've seemed more relaxed these last few days."

"I don't know, Michael. I can't help it. I've been having really weird feelings since we got here. Lots of things seem really familiar—Dave, Jeevan, even Dahlia. Like I've been in this same situation before. Is it crazy?" She stood up. "I think I'm supposed to stay. I just feel like I should."

He shook his head and pulled her back to sit beside him. "You often have strange feelings. Doesn't make them real."

"Maybe this is my chance to learn to take care of myself, Michael. Not be so dependent on you. You've told me, oh, so many times. And Dave's right. I'll be safe staying up at Momma Samuel's. She's like a grandmother. She'll protect me." Joanna smiled and gently pulled her hand from Michael's to touch his cheek. "I'll be okay."

Suddenly, a shout sounded right outside their window. "Doan hackle me, mahn. Den me 'ava mash yuh up." They heard a chair clatter against the wood floor.

Joanna sprang up and stared wide-eyed at the window. "Who's that?"

"I don't know." Michael held the curtain back to glance out. "There's nobody there."

"I did hear that, didn't I?"

"Yeah, but there's nobody there now. Weird. Maybe they ran off." Michael dropped the curtain back in place and took Joanna in his arms. "Crazy, right? Are you okay?"

She nodded. "Do you think they were talking about us?"

"Of course not. Why would they be? Probably just somebody stumbling out of High Hat's." Michael tucked a stray strand of hair behind Joanna's ear. "Listen, I mean it. You don't have to stay here alone. Come home with me."

Joanna's heart pounded like a reggae beat inside her. She felt light-headed as if she were standing at the top of a long staircase. She imagined herself leaping out into the air and floating to the bottom like the dream she often had as a child. She felt the same thrill now, but tinged with a stomach-sinking fear. Still, something shifted ever so slightly inside her at the memory of that soaring flight, that freedom. She moved away from Michael's embrace. "I think I need to stay." She reached up to kiss him, then pulled him toward the door. "Besides, maybe Dave will come back." She thought she saw Michael wince slightly. "Don't worry. I can handle it."

CHAPTER NINE

T he few days before Michael left passed like a dream. Jamaica and the coming separation worked magic on their relationship. Michael spent every moment by her side, as attentive as a suitor, just as she hoped he would. All the pain and doubt of the last ten days seemed to disappear, and she luxuriated in his attention. They spent the days exploring the coves of the cliffs together, happy to be alone, and enjoying their adventures as if storing them up for the time they would be apart.

Now, Joanna sat high on the edge of a cliff above a cove. The water gleamed so clear she could see the fish swimming among the swaying seaweed on the bottom. A group of Jamaican boys took turns jumping from the cliffs across the cove into the sparkling water below. From where she sat, the sea seemed to go on forever. She thought about how far away across the ocean Michael would soon be and a cold chill ran through her. She rubbed her arms up and down to warm herself under the hot sun.

Michael stood nearby, camera in hand. "You look great," he said, moving around her to shoot from different angles. Joanna relaxed and stared down into the water. Michael was just a blur in the corner of her eye, but each time the shutter clicked, she could feel his eyes touching her, caressing her. He knelt down. "It's going to be hard to leave you. I didn't expect that."

"You don't have to go." Joanna pulled down her visor against the glare of the sun.

Michael reached out and ran his fingers over the curve of her shoulder. "I do. Besides, what about Dave? What if he comes back, and I'm still here? That would be awkward."

She frowned. "I'm not really sure what I would do. I doubt he'll be back, though."

He pulled her close and kissed her. "Listen, I've had enough sun. What do you say we go back to the room and take a nap?"

Joanna laughed. "How decadent!"

They gathered up their things and walked back to High Hat's. In the hot afternoon air, the bar was deserted and quiet. They bought two Red Stripes and took the beers with them into the room. It was cooler there now that the sun had travelled to the other side of the building. They sat on the bed to drink the beers. Michael rolled a joint, and they smoked it together in silence. Then, taking Joanna's beer and placing it on the nightstand, he pulled her over to him. "Just so you don't forget me," he said and eased her top over her head. They undressed and tumbled together onto the bed, oblivious of the heat, the sweat, or whether the sounds of their lovemaking might carry to the bar next door. Afterwards, they lay in each other's arms and dozed off to nap as the night came on. Joanna slept fitfully, murmuring in dreams haunted by marijuana. Suddenly, she bolted up, calling out for Michael.

He woke and turned to look at her. "What's the matter?"

"I just dreamed about Reggae." She buried her face in her hands. "Michael, the dream was really scary. She was alive, and I saw her lying on the tracks, only it was in Jamaica." Joanna huddled into Michael's arms. "I ran to pull her off. But then I heard a train coming. Only when I looked, it was two giant feet stomping through the trees. And suddenly, I was paralyzed! I couldn't move at all with this monster coming at me! And then a giant hand reached down to grab me." Joanna shuddered. "Then I woke up."

"Jo, it was only a dream." Michael stroked her hair. "You're still upset about the dog. It was probably the ganja that made you dream."

"The scary part was getting paralyzed. I was completely helpless and scared shitless. And when I woke up, I couldn't call you at first like someone was holding me by the throat." She buried her face in his chest. "Michael, maybe it's an omen. Maybe I should come home with you."

He gently pushed her upright and held her at arm's length. "Jo, you're not helpless, and nothing is going to happen if I'm not with you. You're perfectly capable of taking care of yourself without me. You can relax, and read, and lie in the sun. You'll have a good time, and the separation will be good for us both. I'll be working all the time anyway. And besides, you'll have Jeevan and Dahlia to help you out, too, plus Momma Samuel."

She bit on her lip. "Jeevan's okay, but I don't think I can trust Dahlia."

He held her close as they sat on the edge of the bed. The room was strangely silent as if holding its breath. She sighed and pulled away from him. "I'm okay now, I think. I know it was just a dream. It doesn't have to mean anything." She stood up, shook herself, and took his hand. "All right. It's our last night together. Let's go have a nice dinner. I'll be fine. It's silly."

He reached out to touch her cheek. "I do love you, Jo."

She took his hand and kissed it softly.

***

In the clear brightness of the next day, Joanna's fears faded like stars against the light of the sun. They were still there, but she couldn't see them anymore. Michael and she packed their suitcases and loaded them into Clive's car as Jeevan and Clive lounged around smoking a spliff. Jeevan offered the joint to Joanna and Michael as they piled their bags in the car.

"Yuh leavin' yuh woman, mahn?" Jeevan asked Michael. "Yuh no want 'im no more? 'Im look a pretty nice woman to me, mahn."

Michael laughed as he took the joint. "No, man. She's just going to stay a few more weeks. Then she's coming home."

Jeevan poked Clive in the ribs. "Ah no leave woman behind in Jamaica, mahn. Is wicked place for pretty woman, for true."

Clive laughed, thumped his chest, and coughed out the smoke he held in his mouth. Jeevan smiled at his friend and kicked a small stone across the yard with the bare toe sticking out from the hole in his sneaker. He took the spliff from Joanna, his fingers lingering against hers. "Yuh no 'fraid, sistah, to stay widout yuh mahn?" he asked.

"Why should I be afraid?" She rubbed her hand absently against her shorts. "I'll be up there with Momma Samuel, and I'm hoping Dave will be back soon."

"Ohhhhh," Jeevan said, the word trailing off into the crash of a wave behind them. "Dat's good." Jeevan turned to Michael. "Ah watch 'im, mahn. Ah mash up de rude boys, if dey come round. As a god!" He frowned and pursed his mouth in an attempt at seriousness and looked at Clive, who nodded gravely.

"Oh, come on, Jeevan," Joanna said, "Nothing's going to happen. Just keep me supplied with ganja and change my money. I'll be fine." Joanna prayed her words would be true, but something in Jeevan's smile set her nerves on edge. A shadow passed over them. A large black vulture swooped down and perched in a sea grape tree startling them all.

Jeevan stared at Joanna. "John Crow callin', mahn. Dat bad luck. Yuh must take care, yuh know." He turned to Clive. "Come, mahn, we drive de bags up the hill."

Joanna stood still for a moment, dumbstruck by Jeevan's warning and the vulture that still loomed in the tree. But despite her fears, she had already decided to stay, and she was determined to make it work. She slipped her arm into Michael's. "Let's walk up by ourselves."

They strolled along the road, holding hands. Joanna tried not to think about Jeevan's words or how Michael would be gone in minutes. Jeevan and Clive sped past them, and Michael stopped. "I don't know about leaving you alone. Even Jeevan doesn't seem to think it's such a good idea. And what he said about that bird was strange."

"Michael, don't make me nervous. I do it enough myself. I don't need any help from you." She laughed.

He lowered his eyes to the road as they walked. "You know, Jo, I'm feeling way more jealous than I thought I would."

She laughed. "Jealous of who?"

"Um, I don't know … Dave, Jeevan, who knows who you'll meet. Some other tourist."

Dropping his hand, she put her hands on her hips. "Michael, you've got me so confused. You go back and forth like a yoyo. First, you want to leave me with Dave. Then you're jealous and worried I'll hook up with someone else. I wish you would make up your mind. It's like you want to have your cake and eat it, too."

He shook his head and brushed the hair out of his eyes. "I know, Jo, I'm confused, too. I didn't expect to feel this way." He took her hand again. "I just want you to remember, Jo, you're still with me."

"Well, to tell you the truth," she kissed him lightly, "I'm scared but also sort of excited. Like I'm going on some kind of grand adventure." She pulled away, but he held her. "Come on," she said, "Let's get up to Momma Samuel's before Jeevan and Clive leave without you."

When they reached the cottage, Jeevan and Clive stood politely making conversation with Momma Samuel. They towered over the sturdy little woman, hands folded like schoolboys, listening respectfully to her comments. Several young girls stood off to the side, giggling quietly behind raised hands, not daring to look at the young men. Seeing Joanna and Michael, Momma Samuel shooed the girls away like the chickens that pecked and scratched everywhere in the yard.

"Good day, good day," Momma Samuel said, nodding to Joanna and dipping slightly at the knees. "Yes, yes, is good. Dave tell me yuh soon come. Dat nice. Glad to have yuh, missy. Mek yuhself to home."

Turning to Michael, she said, "Yuh must leave Jamaica now. Yuh must go bahk home. Dat's sad. Jamaica too nice to leave too soon, for true. Ah t'inkin' long time, she gonna stay here. Ah take good care of yuh missus. Only good t'ings gonna happen here for 'im." Momma Samuel raised her hands as if blessing the two of them. "Go now."

Joanna and Michael disappeared into the cool of the house to the room where Joanna's bags lay tumbled on the bed.

"She seems really eager to have you. It's almost like she knew I'd be leaving. It sounded more like an order than a question, didn't it?" Michael opened a drawer in the dresser and peered in.

"Yeah, it's weird. the first time I met her, she said something about me staying here soon. I thought it was strange then, but here I am. Maybe it's fate." Joanna laughed nervously.

Michael walked over and surrounded Joanna in a bear hug. "Well, at least, you'll be safe with that mother hen." He kissed her and pulled her down onto the bed among the luggage.

She returned his kiss, then pushed him gently away. "Michael, you're crazy. You're going to miss your plane."

He kissed her again and rolled from on top of her. "Yeah, you're right. I guess I have to go." They stood up and straightened their clothing. Michael stuck his hands in his pockets and looked around the room, reluctant to leave.

"I'll be fine." Joanna gave him a pat on the backside. "Now, git!"

"Yeah, well, you don't have to be that eager to see me go."

"I'm not, but this is your idea and, Michael," she ran her hand over his cheek, "I'm going to prove to us both that I can live without you."

"Yeah, I guess I deserve that," he said.

Jeevan and Clive waited in the car. Michael slid into the back seat and leaned out the window. "I love you," he said.

Joanna bent down to kiss him. "I love you, too. Write!"

When the car was out of sight, a flood of nausea washed over Joanna, pulling her down like an ocean undertow. She rocked slightly, faint from the sensation. Then wiping tears away with the back of her hand, she turned and walked toward the empty house.

***

Within a few days of Michael's leaving, Joanna settled into a comfortable routine. She rose early in the morning for breakfast, usually bread and butter, some fruit, and instant coffee, heated on the kerosene stove, a smaller version of the one she had seen at Jeevan and Dahlia's. After her meal, she waited for Hosea the ice man to bring her a block of ice for the cooler where she stored her Red Stripes, butter, and a few other perishables. He was a wizened old man whose gums worked constantly in his toothless mouth. Each day, they shared pleasantries, Hosea usually making a prediction about whether it would rain that afternoon.

"Look like it might rain today," he said. "Yuh be nice nice snug in Momma Samuel's house. No rude boys come 'round dis place."

Joanna laughed. "Thanks, Hosea. Momma Samuel's taking good care of me."

Each day when Hosea left, Joanna mounted the bicycle she rented from one of Momma Samuel's grandsons and rode to the market at the center of town. About twenty stalls were set up permanently in the square with produce and house wares. By now, Joanna had settled on several merchants she liked to do business with. She avoided the ones who hustled her and went instead to those stands where she could pick and choose produce for herself. She saw one or two other tourists and smiled at them but didn't stop to talk. Since Michael had left, Joanna had been avoiding other tourists. She was content to eat and sleep and live among the Jamaicans at Momma Samuel's, and it seemed almost fickle, or maybe insulting, to seek companionship among the other Americans when she had the company of the Jamaicans. It was crazy, but she was still waiting for Dave. She knew he probably wouldn't be back, but she enjoyed the romantic notion, anyway.

After the market, Joanna biked back to Momma Samuel's, visions of dinner in her head. Jeevan was waiting for her on the porch. She was glad to see him. He had been as good as his word and visited her often to see how she was getting along. He changed money for her on the black market, bringing her a much better rate than she got at the bank, and kept her supplied with marijuana.

"Ah come to check yuh, mahn," he said. "Yuh need somet'ing? Money? Ah doan get the ganja yet. Maybe come tomorrow."

"That's fine, Jeevan. I can wait. How's it going with Dahlia and Christopher?"

"Dahlia doan matter, mahn. De boy good." He moved to the basket on the bike and grabbed the net bag that held her groceries. "Maybe yuh cook me dinner? Ah cook yuh dinner last time."

"Jeevan! Dahlia cooked dinner."

"Doan matter, mahn. Ah put dat food on table, not de womahn."

"Okay. Whatever you say. I'll cook you both dinner sometime, but I'm sure it won't be hot enough for you guys."

He took the food inside and pulled up a chair by the kitchen table while she put the vegetables and fruits in the cabinet. She liked having Jeevan visit. It made her feel safer. She had met several other young men through one of Momma Samuel's grandsons and soon realized that any foreign woman living alone among Jamaicans was not only an oddity but extremely desirable. In the first three days she was alone, at least four young men had invited her on dates. Jeevan's visits were a bit of a buffer for her.

"Do you want a beer?" she asked.

"No, mahn. If yuh no gonna feed me, Ah must go."

She laughed. "Okay, maybe next time."

CHAPTER TEN

After dinner, Joanna often sat on the porch watching the dusk settle like a mist on the children playing in the dooryard. The crickets began their chorus, and a slight, muggy breeze lapped at her skin, wicking away the sweat of the day. As usual, the faintest beat of reggae floated from a house nearby. She sipped on a Red Stripe and thought of the afternoon she and Dave had sat here, watching the same youngsters. But as she sat alone, panic rose clutching at her chest, making it hard for her to focus. Should she just pack up and go home to Michael? Deep in her dusky melancholy, she didn't notice the young man who came to stand in front of her in the deepening evening.

"Yuh deep t'inkin', mahn. What yuh t'inkin' so?"

She jumped when he spoke. In the darkness, she couldn't make out his features, but his voice sounded familiar. "Who is it?" she called.

"It Wesley, mahn. Ah mek yuh acquaintance dis mornin' wid Philip."

"Philip?"

"Yeh, mahn, Philip. 'Im Momma Samuel gran'son."

The words seemed to come from a disembodied spirit. Joanna could barely see his outline in the darkness. She thought for a moment, trying to put the name to a face. "Oh, Philip. Sure, I remember. Just this morning, right?"

"Yeh, mahn. Sure, mahn." A hint of irritation tinged the free-floating voice.

"Here, let me get a light so we can see." She went inside the house, returning with a lantern. "How can I remember you if

I can't even see you." She laughed and held the light above her head, so it cast its glow on the dark shadow of the man. "That's better. Yeah, I recognize you. Did you say, Wesley?"

"Yeh, mahn, Wesley."

Joanna saw now that the voice belonged to a handsome young man not more than seventeen years old. His face was smooth and hairless, but his eyes seemed to project experience that belied his boyish face. He wore a mesh shirt, revealing a slim torso. She set the lantern on the floor, and suddenly Wesley was on the porch towering over her. She drew back. He stood so close she caught a strong whiff of cologne. She backed away and scratched at her arm. "Geez," she said. "The mosquitos are really biting tonight, aren't they? I'll be right back. I need some Destroyer. You wait here, okay?" She prayed he wouldn't follow her. Back outside, she lit the coil of repellent and placed it on the floor next to the lantern. Wesley had made himself at home, sprawled on one of the chairs.

He asked again, "Whad yuh t'inkin' so deep on?"

She bent over to blow on the punk until it glowed orange and began to smoke heavily. "There, now it's going," she said and sat down. She was not about to tell this man that she was thinking about her boyfriend. "So, did you come to visit Philip? Is he around?"

He didn't answer but seemed to be carefully considering his words. "No, mahn," he said, "Ah only come to look by yuh." He watched to see the effect his words would have on her.

She was flattered. She was at least ten years older than he was. But something set her nerves on edge. She decided to ignore his obvious come on. "Do you live around here, Wesley?"

"Sure, mahn. Ah live right de other side of yuh house." He pointed around the side of the porch.

"You mean here with Momma Samuel's family?" She reached for her Red Stripe but saw the bottle was empty.

He smirked. "No, mahn. Ah live t'ru de bushes, over dere."

She squirmed in her chair and swatted at a mosquito. "Wow, that's close." Putting on her most polite conversation voice, she asked, "Are you still in school?"

At this, he practically crowed. "School? Ah tellin' yuh me workin', mahn. Ah workin' at de Sea Shack."

Joanna knew the place, a small group of tourist cottages nestled into the cliffs a few miles up the road. He told Joanna he had landed the job because he was friends with the man who owned the cottages. He liked it because he got to meet lots of Americans.

"'Merican lady give me dis," he said, stretching out his wrist to show Joanna a crystal-studded watch on a gold band.

She took his arm in her hand and held the watch closer to the lantern. "Nice. A friend of yours?"

"Sure, mahn. Ah got plenty 'Merican friends, plenty 'Merican lady friends," he said, smiling a salesman's smile.

The music from a nearby cottage stopped, and in the quiet, the chirping of insects filled the night. Their clatter ebbed and flowed, reaching a crescendo, then fading into a low, almost electric buzz. The toads kept up their own complaints, in counterpoint to the insects. The muggy air rested like a damp blanket over Joanna. She grabbed her empty bottle and tilted it toward Wesley. "I need another beer. Want one?"

"Sure, mahn."

Back outside, she handed him the beer. "It's not real cold. Sorry," she said.

Wesley nodded and took a long swig of the Red Stripe. "Ah like Guinness bettah. Stout put it bahk." He laughed. Beer in hand, he told Joanna about his job at the Sea Shack. He was a handyman, doing odd jobs around the cottages and running errands for the owner. He also sold the tourists ganja and changed their money.

Joanna didn't mind the conversation, something to pass the evening away, and she offered him a second beer. By now the children were long gone from in front of the porch, and the compound had settled in for the night, like the kids themselves. Several lights burned dimly in the other houses, casting wavering shadows like dark spirits through open doors and windows. Otherwise, the yard was deserted.

"You wouldn't happen to have some ganja on you?" Joanna asked. She was out. She had been expecting Jeevan to come by with some that day, but she hadn't seen him.

"Sure, mahn," Wesley said, grinning again. "Yuh ganja finish? Ah keepin' some in my house. We must go dere and smoke." He stood up and stepped toward the porch stairs. "Come, we smoke, now." He held out his hand to Joanna.

She thought what an idiot she was. Now she would have to go with this kid she barely knew through the dark bush. But she wanted to get high, so she followed him down the steps and around the back of the house where he led her sure-footed through her backyard to an opening in the bush she had never seen, even in the daylight. Taking her hand, he guided her through the undergrowth. The night seemed to enshroud the path, making it as black as the sky. He led her quickly and easily along the path to a gap in the bushes that opened onto a clearing as suddenly as a curtain rising. Here she saw the dark outline of several shacks, lit from within by the glow of lanterns, more shady spirits dancing on the walls inside. The scene had a magical quality, and she imagined secret rites going on by the light of the dim lamps. The chirping of the crickets and the jangling of the tree frogs seemed to vibrate through the air, sending a chill down Joanna's back. Wesley stopped before a tiny, dark hut and stooped to enter through its low doorway. Once in, he turned and motioned for Joanna to follow.

"What's this?" she asked, hesitating at the door.

"Dis my house. Ah build dis house wid wood from Sea Shack. De boss 'im doan know. No problem."

"Who lives over there?" she said, pointing to the other buildings. She was stalling, avoiding following him into the shack, which looked more like a chicken coop than a place where someone could live.

"My fadder and sistah and de baby in one house, and my gran'mudder in de uddah. Come, mahn," he said. He held out his hand to her.

Joanna turned to look at the dark bush behind the shack. She could see the light from Momma Samuel's compound like a wel-coming beacon above the black of the shrubs but cringed at the thought of navigating the dark path back to safety. Wesley beck-oned her in again. She stooped to enter, and once inside, as short as she was, she had to bend to avoid the slant roof that barely cleared her head. Wesley lit a lantern and blew out the match, his lips puckered as if in a kiss. He looked at Joanna, keeping his lips pursed long after the match was out. Then slowly, deliberately, he blew her a kiss. Joanna looked away.

The shack was an A-frame so that both sides of the structure fell to the floor on an angle from the point where they joined at the top. By the light of the lantern, Joanna could see all of Wesley's furnishings—a narrow bed and a bureau. There was no room for anything else. The walls that were also the roof were covered with pictures of half-naked women of all races. Quite the Jamaican bachelor pad, she thought, uneasily.

"How yuh like dis house?" Wesley asked.

Joanna considered carefully what she could say and settled for, "It's very cozy."

Wesley sat on the small bed and patted a spot next to him. "Here, yuh must sit here, mahn."

Joanna hesitated, then sat down, keeping as far from Wesley as she could in the tiny space. He took a small tin can from a drawer in the bureau and rolled a spliff. She watched him, won-dering what she was doing here and how she could get out. She knew she should try to relax. After all, she wanted to experience the real Jamaica, and this was certainly it. "Where do you cook and get washed?" she asked, hoping to ease herself into this new adventure.

"Up to my gran'mudder house," he said, licking the huge joint to seal it. "'Im 'ave a real toilet. 'Im plenty rich lady," he said proudly. "'Im cookin' for me every day."

He put the spliff to his mouth and leaned against the back wall of the shack, stretching his legs out in front of him on the bed. He kicked his sandals off so that his bare feet touched Joanna's thigh. There was no room to pull away in the cramped space.

Then tilting his pelvis up, he smiled and lit a match on his fly zipper. Drawing heavily, he seemed to suck the flame into the spliff, letting it flare up like a tiny torch as he blew the smoke out of his mouth. He smoked until the joint was a third gone, then handed it to Joanna. She took one drag and held the smoke in her lungs.

"No need to hold de smoke, mahn. Yuh 'Mericans very funny." His eyes had become tiny slits, puffed like a prize fighter's. He nodded his head, chuckling. "Dere's plenty ganja. Yuh must smoke it like a cigarette, mahn. Smoke it."

He took Joanna's hand and raised it with the joint to her mouth. She inhaled again on the ganja, drawing the smoke in and letting it out. She took several more drags and handed it back.

Wesley pushed the spliff towards her. "What de matter, mahn? Ah feel yuh 'fraid to smoke. Dis good Jamaican ganja. Plenty pure."

She smoked some more to appease him and handed it to him again. As she did, her attention was captured by the patterns of the flickering shadows on the walls all around her. As she watched, entranced, the patterns began to take on the shape of crawling things, lizards and insects. The rasping of the night insects rose in pitch until it became a buzz she felt in her bones. She felt something on her back. Frantic, she turned to look at the wall behind her, sure that she would find it teeming and alive with bugs. She saw only the sputtering shadows cast by the lantern. She forced herself to breathe deeply, slowly, and turned back toward Wesley.

He smiled languidly at her. "Ah feel yuh getting' plenty high on dis ganja, mahn. Dis special ganja, Christmas ganja from when de plants first come ripe. Ah takin' de buds, mahn, 'cause dey 'ave," he paused, "special power. Dey cost plenty plenty money. 'Merican friend, 'im mek me a present at Christmas."

His voice seemed to travel to Joanna over a very long distance as if wafting on a breeze. She watched Wesley's lips moving, but the sounds she heard were out of sync, like a movie soundtrack out of phase with the picture. She caught the words "special power," and the sing-song lilt of Wesley's voice, coming from far away, sounded like an incantation, like the words of a spell he was casting. His face turned waxy, began to melt in the hot, orange light of the lantern, and in a panic, Joanna flung her hands to her own face to check the solidness of her flesh. She looked toward the women on the walls, but they, too, had begun to melt, their flesh oozing toward her. Soon she would be covered in the hot liquid of their bodies. She gasped. Her heart hammered, and she gagged on the smoke that filled the air.

"Wesley, I've got to go," she said, standing up and whacking her head on the low ceiling. She fell back on the bed.

"No, mahn. Yuh must stay. We 'ave a good time, now, mahn."

"I can't. I've got to go." She moved toward the door.

He shot out his hand and grabbed her arm, pulling her down onto the bed. "Ah feel me must show yuh somet'ing," he said.

Still holding her firmly, he reached over to the dresser and opened a drawer with his other hand. He rummaged around, searching for something underneath his clothes. Then he turned to smile at Joanna. "Now, yuh see what a bad mahn Ah am."

Slowly he pulled a dark metal object from the drawer. Bringing it into the light, he released Joanna from his grip to run his hand lovingly over a pistol.

Joanna scrambled away, eyes riveted to the gun, disbelieving. "Wesley, what are you doing?"

"Doan be vexed wid no fear, mahn. Ah not hurt yuh. Ah keepin' dis for de rude boys."

Joanna felt a tightening around her chest, rising like a hand to her neck. "What rude boys?" She squeezed the words through the stranglehold on her throat.

"De rude boys who comin' after me ganja. Ah must carry protection."

He held the gun towards her, offering to let her hold it. She could feel her pulse pounding in the veins in her neck. "No, that's okay," she said and scrunched into the wall away from the gun.

He laughed, closed his eyes, and threw back his head. "Mahn, dis a fake gun, just mek-believe. Ah mekin' a joke on yuh. De smart 'Mericans, dey believe everyt'ing Jamaicans tell dem. Yuh like a baby." He rocked back and forth, the gun in his hand, rising and falling with his movements. Joanna kept her eyes on the pistol as if watching it made it somehow less dangerous.

Wesley quieted down and wiped the tears from his eyes. He pulled a piece of cloth from the drawer, wrapped the gun in it, and buried it back in the dresser. When he had closed the drawer, Joanna slid off the bed and, stooping now, moved toward the door. She heard him call to her as she stepped outside.

"Ah check yuh tomorrow, for true," he said.

She walked quickly away from the hut and the surrounding bush toward the other houses. She was grateful for the dark because it covered her retreat from Wesley, but she was petrified of its palpable denseness. There was no way she was walking through the bushes back to Momma Samuel's. She saw what looked like a path and hoped it would lead to the road. "Great," she said out loud, "Now all I have to do is walk all alone in the dark on the road. Can't wait."

She wished desperately that she had had the sense to bring a flashlight with her. But, then, suddenly, as if from nowhere, she was surrounded by barking, yelping dogs, nipping at the air around her. She froze, paralyzed. Images of train tracks, a dog's body, a giant foot, flashed in her mind. Her dream! She forced herself to move, inching slowly past the nearest house, the dogs keeping their distance but not leaving her side.

"I'm going. I'm going," she whispered to the dogs. As she came even with the door, someone stuck their head out and held a lantern high.

"Who dere?" came an old woman's voice. The dogs' yelping quieted some.

"It's Joanna. I was visiting Wesley."

"Dat gran'boy," said the woman, her voice high-pitched and scratchy. "'Im got no sense to mek yuh walk alone t'ru de dogs. Yuh wait dere."

The old woman hobbled down the steps towards Joanna. Her

features were hidden by the shadows. Only her hunched form was visible as the dogs skulked over to her. "Good dogs," she said. "How yuh get in here, anyway? De dogs doan bark when yuh come in."

"We came through the bushes from Momma Samuel's."

The old woman stopped and held the lantern up so the light fell on Joanna. "Oh, Momma Samuel's. Ah hear 'bout 'Merican girl 'im stayin' wid Momma Samuel. Yuh de girl?"

"Yes, I've been there a few days."

"Yuh friend? Yuh doan hear word of 'im?"

News travels fast, Joanna thought. "Not yet," she answered.

"Ah feel 'im not soon come bahk," the woman said, shining the light on the path in front of them. A lizard slithered across and scurried into the bushes. "Here, Ah must walk wid yuh to de road. De dogs doan stop dere barkin' if Ah doan do so." She began to walk, but slowly, as if her bare feet were sore. Joanna followed, breathing more easily again.

When they neared the ocean road, the old woman stopped. "Ah holding de light for yuh, and de moon rising some now. Yuh find yuh way easy. Just de next road over. Close, close."

Joanna thanked her and started down to the ocean road in the dim glow of the old woman's light. When Joanna was in sight of the ocean, the woman called from above, "Doan mess none wid Wesley, girl. 'Im be me gran'baby, but 'im crazy bad boy."

Turning, the woman disappeared into the bushes like a phantom, leaving Joanna in the dark once more, with just the faint glow of the bobbing lantern visible above the bushes. Sighing, she looked up to see the moon scuttle behind a cloud. She walked quickly down the middle of the road, avoiding the dense bush to her left. The ocean murmured at her right with the mutterings of a sea full of souls. She turned often to look over her shoulder but saw only the darkness closing behind her like a black curtain. The moonlight, too weak to light her way, cast smoky shadows that fluttered and wavered in the corners of her eyes, making her start at each wisp of the wind through the sea-grape trees. She hurried along, imagining that at any moment something dark and smothering might jump from the bushes.

As she neared the turnoff to the compound, she thought she saw a figure moving toward her. She stopped, hoping it was just another shadow waving in the wind. But no, there was definitely something or someone coming toward her. She looked to the bush, thought of hiding there but that was no better than facing whatever was in front of her. Slowly, the thing began to form itself into a human being, a man. She tried to quiet the pounding in her ears, breathing deeply. She told herself it was ridiculous to be so afraid. It was just another person walking home late at night. But still her heart thumped, and her breath came in raspy spurts. She began walking toward the person, thinking, for a brief, sane moment, how foolish she must look standing dead still in the middle of the road. By now, the man was within a few feet of her and heading directly at her, not moving to the side to pass. Her every muscle tensed. She was ready to run if he came any closer. She still could not make out his dark features in the murky light. Then she heard him.

"I-ree, Joanna. Wah gwaan?"

He knew her name. Was it Wesley with his gun? Did he double around to get in front of her? She shuddered, her whole body trembling. "Who is it?" she whispered.

"Yuh doan know Ah, for true? It Jeevan, mahn."

She almost collapsed like a balloon as the fear went out of her. She had never been so happy to see anyone. She moved forward and grabbed him by both arms, ready to hug him, but instead she said, "Jeevan, I'm so glad it was you. I was scared shitless." She dropped her hands to her sides. "How did you know it was me in this pitch black."

He laughed. "Yuh funny, mahn. Yuh not pitch black. Yuh white, yuh know. It easy to see yuh."

She laughed and relaxed a bit. "Right! But how did you know it was me and not somebody else?"

"No udder crazy white girl living by 'imself 'round here."

She felt a strange mix of conflicting emotions roiling inside her. She wanted desperately to ask him to walk her home. But would it sound like a come on? She could feel him beginning to fidget as if he were getting ready to walk on. She wanted to reach out, take his arm. Her hand rose on its own, but she forced it down. She tried to think of something to say to keep him there. Then, remembering the ganja he had promised, she said, "Jeevan, did you get any smoke for me?"

"No, mahn, de mahn no come today. Ah come to look by yuh to tell yuh dat."

"You were up at Momma Samuel's?"

"Sure, mahn, Ah waiting on yuh long, long time. Where yuh be, mahn, so late in de night?" There was a strange, petulant tone in his voice, disapproving, almost paternal.

"Wesley came by. A friend of Momma Samuel's grandson …"

Jeevan interrupted, "Ah know de mahn." His annoyance surprised Joanna.

"Well, I asked him if he had some ganja, and he said he had some at his place. So, we went over to get high …"

"'Im a bad mahn," Jeevan said in a low voice, filling Joanna with foreboding. "Hear what Ah telling yuh, mahn. Yuh must stay far, far away from 'im."

Joanna shivered. Wesley's own grandmother had warned her, too. How close had she come to actual harm? Again, she saw the gun in Wesley's hand. An owl screeched close by sending an electric shock through her body.

"You're right. He showed me a gun."

"A gun!" Jeevan practically jumped into the air. "De boy 'ave a gun? Bomboclatt! 'Im t'ink 'im a rude boy! Dis mahn plenty vexed. 'Im crazy!"

Joanna forgot about appearances and clutched at Jeevan's arm. "Jeevan, will you walk me home? I'm scared to walk alone."

In the dim glow of the moon, Joanna could barely make out the grin that covered Jeevan's face, but she sensed a softening about him as if her question had released some tension in him.

"Sure, mahn," he said, his voice soft, almost caressing. "Ah protect yuh, mahn. Ah walkin' yuh home, for true. Ah promise yuh mahn Michael, right? Doan fret 'bout it no more."

They walked in silence up the road, making a turn at the dirt path leading to Momma Samuel's. The bushes, so close to the path here, blocked out most of the moon's feeble light. Joanna shuddered to think of walking up alone and was so grateful to have Jeevan for company that she felt the urge to take his hand. As if reading her mind, he reached out and took hers in his own warm, rough hand. "Here, give Ah yuh hand. It plenty dark here. Ah know de way good."

The touch of his skin seemed to drain the fears from Joanna, and she felt as if, together, they were enclosed in a protective bubble. She let him guide her through the blinding darkness until she could see several lights glowing above them in the compound, giving her back her sense of direction. She dropped her hand from his.

They reached her porch and went into the house. Jeevan flicked his lighter so Joanna could find the lantern sitting on a low table. She brought it over to him to light. Then as he held the lantern above her head, she walked from room to room to light a lantern in each.

"Dat is truly plenty plenty light," Jeevan said, laughing.

She smiled, and grabbing two lukewarm Red Stripes from the cooler, led him back to the porch. She lit another punk for the mosquitoes, and they sat silent, sipping on the beers.

"Jeevan," Joanna began, her voice thick, "do you think Wesley might try to break in tonight while I'm sleeping? He lives right through the bushes."

He didn't answer right away but studied Joanna's face carefully. Finally, he shook his head slowly. "Hmmm, no, mahn. Ah doubtin' 'm bodder yuh here at Momma Samuel."

Only slightly relieved by his answer, Joanna sat brooding, listening to the din of the frogs and crickets rise and fall. The lantern in the shack next to hers went out, casting the area to the side of the porch into complete darkness. A lone dog howled into the night far off in the distance. She suddenly wished she could invite Jeevan to spend the night although it would be an act of desperation rather than passion, she knew.

He bent forward, carelessly flicking at a moth that battered itself against the glass of the lantern. Straightening up, he turned toward Joanna. "Tomorrow Jamaica Independence Day."

His words were so far from Joanna's thoughts that, at first, she didn't understand what he had said. When she didn't answer, he went on, "It a holiday for all Jamaica people."

Joanna collected her thoughts enough to speak. "A holiday? That's cool. Does that mean nobody has to work?"

"For true, mahn. Everybody go to de beach and swim on Independence Day." He paused. "Yuh want to ride on me motorbike and go to de beach?"

Joanna was totally unprepared for his invitation. What about Dahlia and the baby Christopher? "Well, I'm sure Dahlia wouldn't like that," she said, stammering to get the words out.

"'Im gone. 'Im go back to 'im family in de hills," he said sullenly.

"She did? What about Christopher?"

"'Im took de baby wid."

"When is she coming back?"

Jeevan shrugged and made a motion of washing his hands. That small gesture seemed to express all his feelings for the woman. Joanna thought of how he had treated Dahlia at dinner. She certainly couldn't blame her for leaving to go back to her family. Joanna imagined she would have been long gone herself if Michael had ever acted that badly.

"Well, mahn. Whad yuh say? Yuh will go wid me?"

Joanna hesitated. Was it okay if Dahlia had really left him? She and Jeevan were friends after all, and it was only a ride to the beach. When was she ever going to get another chance to celebrate Jamaican Independence Day? She nodded. "Well, if you're sure it's okay, I'll go." He smiled, but she had the sense that she was diving head-first into a deep pool.

CHAPTER ELEVEN

Jeevan roared up to Momma Samuel's around ten the next morning like a Hell's Angel, complete with mirror sunglasses and a shining black and chrome motorcycle. Despite the heat, he wore a black leather vest over his t-shirt. The noise of the bike seemed to bring every child from miles around scurrying to Joanna's porch. Some of the older boys and young men stood farther back, lounging casually as if uninterested in the shiny machine. Joanna caught sight of Wesley, who winked at her as if sharing a secret. She nodded slightly, then turned toward Jeevan. The kids were shouting and scrambling around the bike, giving the scene a circus air. Joanna walked over and ran her hand over the smooth cover of the seat.

"Nice bike," she said. "When did you get it?" She hadn't ever seen him on a motorcycle before.

"Bike broke before, mahn," Jeevan said. "Ah doan 'ave money to buy de part to fix it up. Ah got de money now."

He reached over to smack one of the kids' hands away from the bike. Grinning, he bent forward and huffed on the spot the child had touched. He pulled out the bottom of his shirt and rubbed the imaginary smudge from the chrome handlebars. Then he threw his leg over the bike and motioned Joanna to get on. When she was settled firmly on the back, her sunglasses shading her eyes, he revved the bike up and took off with a lurch, scattering the kids behind them. Joanna jerked backward, precariously close to falling off.

Jeevan turned his head to the side to make himself heard over the din of the motor. "Yuh must hold on, mahn," he shouted, "else yuh fall, for true."

They turned off Momma Samuel's road onto the ocean road. Joanna's heart jumped when Jeevan pulled onto the left side of the road. What was he doing? She clutched her arms around his waist until she was pressed close to his back. Her eyes watered. Her hair snapped in the wind. But she laughed when she remembered that Jamaicans drive on the left. The bike vibrated between her legs as they sped along spewing dust behind them. She tingled with an exhilaration that seemed to lift her into the air until she felt as if she were soaring. She imagined kicking her legs out to let them flutter behind her with her arms wrapped around Jeevan. "Fun," she yelled above the wind just as Jeevan took the bike into a curve.

"Lean!" he hollered as the bike dipped within inches of the dirt road. For a second, Joanna lost sight of the sky and saw only gravel coming at her face. She closed her eyes, but then the bike was upright again, and Jeevan was laughing into the air. They sped along the ocean road, people, trees, buildings just a blur of color. Joanna hung on even more tightly to Jeevan's waist, not caring what he was thinking. The thrill of the ride held her completely. It was the most exciting thing she had ever done.

As they approached the round-about in the center of town, Jeevan slowed down. "We must watch for Babylon," he called over his shoulder.

"The police?"

"Yeh, mahn. De police."

As he pulled out of the turn onto an open stretch of paved road, he let out the clutch and shot into high gear. The bike took off like a bucking horse, throwing Joanna backward so hard that her hands loosened around Jeevan's waist. Quickly pulling one hand from the handlebars, he grabbed for her free hand and held her until she could clasp her hands again. She held on so tightly now that she had to turn her head sideways and rest her cheek on his shoulder to keep from burrowing her nose in his neck.

"Jeevan, you're crazy," she yelled, laughing.

"Yeh, mahn. Jeevan crazy," he shouted, letting the last word trail into the wind that streamed past their heads.

They were coming to a curve in the road where a large boulder obstructed their view of oncoming traffic. Just as they were about to lean into the turn, a small car came careening around the bend, people, arms, heads, waving out all four windows. Jeevan swerved to avoid a collision, and the rear of the bike fishtailed out. Joanna closed her eyes again and buried her face in Jeevan's shirt. They swayed from side to side as Jeevan struggled to get control. She wished she had a helmet. Finally, the bike stabilized, and she opened her eyes. She gulped air and tightened her legs to stop their shaking.

"Jeevan, maybe we should slow down a little," she said, lips pressed to his ear.

"Okay, mahn. We almost dere anyhow. Enjoy de ride."

In a few minutes, they pulled up to a section of the road where a dozen bikes were parked. Jeevan held the bike steady while Joanna hopped off. Her body still trembled from her fright and the bike's vibrations, and her legs wobbled as she tried to stand. They stepped onto the beach, winding their way through the bodies that lay everywhere on the narrow strip of glittering sand. The shore stretched for miles on either side, the crystal blue water lapping softly at its edge. Jeevan led Joanna to a little spot of unclaimed sand, strutting before her. She felt as if the eyes of every Jamaican were on her. She saw two other tourists sitting side by side on a towel, a man with a ponytail down to his shoulders and a woman wearing a large peace symbol on a necklace. She nodded in reply to their wave. As far as she could tell, there were no other tourists on the beach. She felt suddenly out of place, like some strange specimen brought out for show.

Jeevan spread the blanket on the hot sand. He stepped out of his pants, revealing a pair of bathing trunks underneath. He dropped his vest and pulled his t-shirt over his head. Strong, smooth muscles held his stomach taut. His torso was brown, but his biceps and thighs had darkened from the sun.

She hesitated before removing her own shorts and top. Her skin was so pale even after hours under the Jamaican sun. Rummaging in her bag for her suntan oil, she sat down next to Jeevan on the blanket. She began to spread the lotion onto her skin when Jeevan reached out to stop her.

"Doan put dat on yuh skin," he said in an undertone. She looked at him, eyebrows raised. "Dese people doan carry faith wid dis kind of t'ing," he said, motioning toward the people lying closest to their blanket.

"What do you mean?"

"Dese people t'ink it foolishness to put de oil on yuh skin. Dat somet'ing yuh must do in yuh house, not before udder people."

Joanna shook her head and scowled. "But I'll burn to a crisp in no time."

He laughed and pulled at the skin on his forearm. "Dis skin doan burn." He shrugged and looked away when she began to rub in the oil again.

It was absurd to be uptight about using suntan oil. She was not going to burn just to save Jamaican sensibilities. She slathered the oil onto her shoulders, thinking about the day on the cliffs with Dave, remembering the feel of him smoothing lotion on her back. She stopped, the open tube over her outstretched hand. She hadn't thought of Dave or Michael all day, in fact, not once since Wesley had appeared last night. Was that a good thing or a bad thing? She wasn't sure. But what could she do? She was here with Jeevan, and the others were far away. And wasn't that what Michael had wanted? For her to be more independent? Well, she was certainly being that. She smiled and finished spreading the lotion, then turned to Jeevan. "What about tourists? Haven't these people ever seen other tourists use suntan oil?"

"No, mahn. Dese people come from de hills. Dey doan see much tourists in de hills."

They lay awhile in the sun without talking, letting the heat burn away the small irritation they felt with each other. Jeevan turned to her and propped himself up on his elbow. "Yuh been to de hills?" he asked.

"No, just on the coast."

He rolled over on his stomach and played with the sand in front of him, letting it run through his fingers in handfuls. "Den yuh must come wid me tonight to de hills. Big dance in de hills." His words sounded not so much like a question as an order.

Joanna swatted at a bug on her thigh. Something inside her thrilled at the way he staked his claim on her. The motorcycle ride, his invitation to the hills, added to a sense of danger, a foreboding that made her squirm. Yet, at the same time, she felt an unusual lightness, something she didn't know she had been missing.

He dusted the sand from his hands and leaned close to Joanna. "Yuh come?" he asked.

She raised her hand to shade her eyes and looked him squarely in the face. His full lower lip was set in a pout, but his put-on look of innocence still warmed her. She broke into a smile despite herself. "Okay. Sounds like fun. Sure, I'll go."

They spent the rest of the morning lolling on the beach, running in and out of the warm ocean, playing in the shallows like two kids out of school. Jeevan ran after Joanna, catching her with a tackle and pulling them both into the surf with a splash. He helped her up, grabbed her around the waist and threw her backwards into the water again. Joanna laughed and shouted with each tumble, unable to remember the last time she had carried on like this. She felt as if layers of wrapping were washing away in the salty sea.

By afternoon, Joanna had had enough of the sun, and since they were both hungry, they packed up their things and headed back to the bike. After a safe, leisurely ride back home, Jeevan dropped Joanna off at Momma Samuel's, saying he had to see a man about some ganja. They made plans for Jeevan to pick her up after dinner to drive to the hills.

When he was gone, Joanna made herself a sandwich, grabbed a Red Stripe out of the cooler, and sat on the porch. She felt great after the sun and the beach and the bike ride home as if a world of new possibilities were opening up before her. Then, from around the back of her house, Wesley materialized. Up close in the daylight, he looked even younger than he had the night before, and Joanna dismissed her night fears as the result of too much marijuana.

"Where yuh been, mahn? Ah come to check yuh t'ree times," he said, as if he had been expecting her. His manner was so brazen that she had to think for a moment whether she had made him some promise last night. But she hadn't. She was sure.

"Wesley, you saw me leave this morning with Jeevan. We went to the beach." She took a bite of her sandwich.

Wesley stood moving around the sandy dirt with his foot. Joanna watched him, hoping she could avoid inviting him onto the porch for a beer.

"When yuh comin' to check on me again?" he asked without meeting her eyes.

"I don't know, Wesley," she said, putting the Red Stripe down on the floor where it would be less obvious. "I've already got plans for tonight."

"But Ah t'inking yuh like me, mahn," he said, glancing up at her shyly. The look irritated Joanna. Last night he had laughed at her fear over the gun. Now he played coy. Yet, some warning inside told her to hide her annoyance.

"Wesley, I do like you, but I have plans. Jeevan and I are going to a dance," she said, hoping to discourage him.

His face clouded over with a scowl, and he began poking in the sand again with his foot, kicking up little wisps of dirt. "Ah t'inking yuh gonna be my girl," he said, locking eyes with Joanna.

She bolted straight up in her chair. "Wesley! We just met. I barely know you!"

Wesley glared at her and spoke in a slow monotone, as if reasoning with a child. "How yuh mean yuh doan know Ah? What yuh know 'bout Jeevan? Ah feel yuh know me plenty good as 'im. What about 'im woman?"

He stood very still as he spoke, but the muscles in his neck strained and knotted. His chest seemed to swell as Joanna watched him. For a moment, she imagined his head popping off like a soda bottle cap under pressure. Shaking her own head, she started to answer but stopped. She didn't owe him an explanation. They faced each other like two boxers waiting for the round to start. Then as if saved by the bell, Joanna heard Momma Samuel calling to Wesley. The tension drained from his neck and body, deflating him like a balloon. He turned, transformed before Joanna's eyes into a meek youth, and looked toward Momma Samuel.

The old woman came up to him, waving her hands in front of her, shooing him away, showering him with a stream of patois Joanna couldn't understand. He hung his head and walked toward the side of the house, then stopped, and turned to Joanna.

"Ah check yuh later," he said, wagging his finger at Joanna with such menace that she shuddered.

"I won't be here," she answered.

"Go. Stop dis ugliness," Momma Samuel said, her high, wavering voice taking on a flinty strength. "Go bahk home, boy, before Ah gettin' plenty plenty angry wid yuh."

He turned and disappeared behind the house.

"Dis boy rude," Momma Samuel said to Joanna when he was gone. "'Im always been makin' trouble, even since 'im only a little boy. 'Im so nice one time, den 'im so bad de next. Yuh must tell me if 'im come 'round bodderin' yuhself."

"Thanks, Momma Samuel. I'll let you know."

The old woman nodded and walked away. Joanna sipped on her beer wondering what she had gotten herself into.

CHAPTER TWELVE

Dusk was falling over the compound when Jeevan returned on his motorcycle. The bike roared like a bull elephant as Jeevan made the turn up the road to Momma Samuel's but soon fell silent. Joanna watched from the porch as he walked the bike up the compound path to the house. Smiling at her, he leaned the bike against the porch and ambled up the steps. He wore a yellow fishnet shirt that clearly revealed his chest. A thick gold watchband accented the rich cocoa of his arm in the dim light. For the first time since Joanna had known him, he had changed his holey sneakers for a pair of high tops, sporting the red, green, and yellow of the Jamaican flag. Even Christopher's baptism hadn't rated that. Joanna smiled at the familiar stars and stripes cap still perched on his head.

"Pretty spiffy," she said, motioning him to sit beside her.

Jeevan frowned. "Speeffy, mahn? What speeffy?"

She laughed. "You look nice."

He grinned, then leaned over and whispered to Joanna, "Ah bring de ganja for yuh." He patted the top of his cap. "Here. Ah holdin' it here."

"All right!" Joanna high-fived him. "Let's get high."

"Shhhhhh, mahn. Yuh doan want Momma Samuel to hear. We must go inside de house to smoke de herb," he said, getting up and leading her by the hand.

Once inside, they smoked, not one joint, but two of the thick spliffs Jeevan rolled. Although Joanna had only one lungful to his four, she was so high she wasn't sure she could ride behind him on the bike. It had grown dark outside, and the small kerosene lantern on the kitchen table cast a weak orange glow over the room. Joanna watched as every shiny surface in the room danced with the glow of the lamp, flickering with tiny points of light. The gold band on Jeevan's wrist caught her eye, gleaming and twinkling whenever he moved his hand. As she concentrated on the dancing rays, she saw the band rise and come toward her, glittering against a dark background until it filled her vision completely. The whole room swam under a sea of warm gold, as Joanna sat engulfed in a world of shimmering, pulsating lights. All around her sparkled and sputtered, casting a magical spell over the small kitchen. She floated in a space where light possessed substance, where a person could travel anywhere on glowing rivers in the time it took to take a breath. She marveled at the beauty of the vision. She wanted to drift forever in this magical, golden moment, to journey on a bright, sparkling sea.

Then, something soft on her face. She jumped. Jeevan's hand, his flesh meshing with hers. In a moment, the glimmering hallucination was gone, and only the lamp light reflected on his watch band. He held his palm to her cheek. His calloused fingertips felt rough on her skin, but real. Jeevan was real, and she knew in that instant that he was not an illusion that would vanish.

"It comin' to de time we must go," he said, speaking low, as if not wanting to break the spell the ganja had cast over her.

She sat mute, then shivered, like a dreamer waking. "Okay." She cleared her throat and smiled. "I guess I'm as ready as I'll ever be."

He rolled another joint and tucked it under his cap. Once outside, Jeevan righted the bike and they walked down the path until they were well beyond the compound. The moon was fuller tonight, throwing enough light to show the way. When they reached the ocean road, Jeevan started the bike and held it steady while Joanna mounted. This time, she didn't have to be told to wrap her arms tightly around his waist. She leaned her cheek against his shoulder, and the fishnet of his shirt pressed against her skin.

They drove slowly down the ocean road. Jeevan took the turns smoothly, and Joanna leaned easily into the curve behind him, feeling their bodies moving together, a single unit with the powerful bike vibrating beneath them. Jeevan didn't push the bike, as if content to glide with no destination in mind. The wind brushed gently against Joanna's face, bringing with it the salty perfume of the ocean, as she watched the seascape slide by.

Soon they were out of town and climbing into the hills. Now that they had left the dim lights of the town behind, the dense bush loomed darkly like a jungle on either side. As Joanna's eyes became accustomed to the moonlight, a soft ease settled over her like an old, comfortable shawl, and the hum of the motor-cycle lulled her into a dream of Michael. She would return to the States and find him waiting eagerly for her. They would be happy again. Maybe she would get pregnant. She felt a warm rush of contentment infusing her like a shot of whiskey, slithering through her, melting her. She imagined she was wrapped around Michael and pulled her body closer to his back.

"Dat nice," Jeevan said. She started slightly but didn't pull away.

She floated in and out of dim fantasies, losing track of time, content to ride forever behind Jeevan. One by one, she noticed little shacks dotting the road, their interiors aglow with warm lights. She stretched upward to put her mouth close to his ear. "Are we there yet?"

"Soon come, mahn." He pursed his lips as if to kiss the wind.

As they neared the outskirts of the small town, Joanna could sense the rumbling beat of reggae as the bike itself seemed to pulse in time to a distant music. There were no streetlights, and the only light came from Jeevan's headlight or the lantern glow from the houses that clustered closer together now. They approached the center of town, and Joanna saw several people strolling in the direction they were riding. Jeevan pulled into a narrow driveway before a building glowing inside and out with orange and red lights.

As Joanna waited for Jeevan to pull out the kickstand, a crowd of people began to form at the door to the dance hall. This was the real Jamaica, not some shiny façade erected to keep tourists entertained. Was she crazy to come all this way with Jeevan when she might not know the rules? She hesitated.

Jeevan turned to her. "Wah gwaan?" he asked.

"I'm a little nervous." She tugged down on her skirt.

"No fear, mahn. Yuh wid me," Jeevan said and walked toward the crowd.

The building slouched long and low with a thatched roof for cover. The walls rose three-fourths of the way up, leaving an open space for the breeze to enter. Joanna stood enthralled as the lights seemed to pulse with the rhythm of the music inside. The small crowd separated as Jeevan neared the entrance, and seeing him disappear into the hall, Joanna snapped out of her trance and ran to catch up. She definitely didn't want to walk in alone. They stopped at a table by the door, and Jeevan paid a few dollars. He snaked his way slowly through the crowd inside without turning back to see if Joanna followed. She felt a little like a harem girl walking ten paces behind her sheik. She grabbed onto the waist of his pants. "Hey, wait for me." He turned and took her hand.

"What's the name of this place?" Joanna asked.

"Grange Hill," Jeevan said. "Ah meet Dahlia first time here."

Joanna's every muscle clenched, and she stood frozen staring at him. Was this Dahlia's hometown? Did he bring her here hoping it would get back to Dahlia?

Jeevan turned back to Joanna. "No fear, mahn. 'Im and me done done." He pulled Joanna with him to a clear spot at the side of the hall. In the dim orange light, Joanna could see the hall was packed. Small groups collected around the edges, but most of the people were on the dance floor or at a make-shift bar at one end of the hall. At the other end, a disk jockey fidgeted with a meager assortment of electronic equipment set up on a table. Beside him, four huge speakers, stacked two to a side, rose above the heads of the dancers, booming out the pounding reggae. Among the couples, Joanna noticed a number of men in dreadlocks dancing alone. Their untamed, matted hair marked them as Rastafarians. Although Joanna had seen Rastas on the coast, by the looks of the dance floor, the hills were where they made their home.

"Ah go now get some Red Stripes. Soon come bahk," Jeevan said. Joanna nodded as he disappeared into the crowd.

One Rasta danced close to where she stood. He shuffled and swayed, not dancing as much as walking to the music. With his head tilted back, his arms swung at his sides, back and forth with the beat. He glided, eyes closed, lips open as if taking in the music through his mouth as well as his ears. There was an ecstatic, erotic quality to his movements that made Joanna uneasy as if she were intruding on some private experience.

Joanna felt exposed standing by herself at the table. She wished she had gone with Jeevan for the beers. She stood up on her toes, straining to see above the bobbing heads on the dance floor. She could sense the eyes of the Jamaicans on her. Several men, standing together against the wall, stared at her brazenly. One of them, a big man, his flowered shirt opened in a vee to the waist, eyed her up and down. Lifting his beer bottle toward her, he smacked his lips and sneered.

She glanced away, letting her eyes wander to a group of women who clustered on the other side of the floor. They chatted among themselves, occasionally glaring at her. She flushed. She looked toward the bar for Jeevan, only to lock eyes again with her hefty admirer. He leered at her and moved in her direction. Her breath caught, and she edged backward, eyes locked on him. Something brushed her leg from behind. Whirling around, she almost fell into the arms of one of the swaying Rastas. He opened his eyes just a slit, smiled at her, and moved away in a reggae reverie. She heard the women across the hall laughing. The sound floated like a poisonous cloud over her. The insistent beat of the music rose through the floor until it seemed to take over the rhythm of her heart. The lights throbbed in time, and for a frightening moment, Joanna felt as if her body had become the music. She shook herself to be sure she could move her own arms. Get control, she whispered.

She needed Jeevan. How could he leave her? The packed floor left no escape from the leering man. Taking a step forward, she tried to skirt his advancing hulk. He reached behind her and grabbed her buttocks through her skirt. She yelped, then grasped his hand, struggling to push it away. Freeing herself, she pivoted around right into Jeevan, slopping beer onto the floor from the bottles he carried. He handed her the beers, and pushing her aside, stuck his face close to the other man's contemptuous grin.

"How yuh getting' so cocky, mahn!" Jeevan said. "Yuh messin' wid a lot of trouble, mahn, when yuh messin' wid me girl."

Joanna flinched. It was stupid for Jeevan to get into a fight over her although sort of sweet in a macho way. She reached for his arm, bottles still in her hands, and tried to pull him away. More beer spilled. He shook her off.

"Is mahn talk we makin'," he said to her.

The big man seemed to swell to two times Jeevan's size. He smiled down at Jeevan. "Yuh makin' a mess of ugliness for a littel boy," he said. He moved closer and put his arm around Jeevan, who fought to shrug him off. The larger man had a clear advantage in strength and succeeded in holding Jeevan. "Littel broddah," he said, in a soothing voice, "Mek no sense in feudin'." With that, he released his grip on Jeevan, pulled a large pen knife from his pants pocket, and proceeded to clean his nails. Jeevan's face slipped into a wide grin. "Go dance wid yuh girl, now, mahn. Ah standin' right here and watchin' yuh," the big man said, his eyes still on his nails.

"Sure, mahn. Ah just jokin' wid yuh, mahn," Jeevan said, inching away. Then taking Joanna's elbow, he walked her to a table on the other side of the floor, took the beers from her, and set them down. When they were out of earshot, the scowl returned to his face. "Bomboclaat," he said, spitting out the curse.

They danced, and within minutes, Jeevan relaxed his scowl and seemed to forget his rival. Rotating his hips and watching Joanna, he seemed intent on the dancing. When Joanna looked again, the man was gone, but she still felt uneasy. She leaned in close to Jeevan so she could be heard above the beat of the reggae. "I don't think these people like me. Maybe because I'm American. Like I don't belong here."

"Doan madder, mahn. Dey just hill folk. Dey jealous 'cause yuh wid me."

She found herself laughing despite her anxiety. "I didn't know you were so popular, Jeevan." The thundering music drowned out her words.

"Whad yuh saying?"

"Nothing." She focused on dancing, trying to mimic the motions of the women around her. Jeevan placed his hands on her hips. She grew warm and fluid under his touch. He guided her until she dipped and swayed in unison with him, their movements matched like two flags waving in a soft breeze. Soon she was not aware of anything except Jeevan. The hall, the other dancers, all faded from her consciousness until Jeevan and she were alone in a cocoon woven by the music, and her body flowed into the slow, sensuous movements without any effort or will on her part. A magical power bound them tightly as if no space existed between them.

Without a word, Jeevan took Joanna's hand and led her out to the bike. She was not sorry to leave the dance. Her anxiety over the other man and the hall full of Jamaicans was still strong, and she longed to speed away on the bike with Jeevan. They slipped onto the seats and took off through the town, traveling the road back to Negril, content in their own private world, wrapped in the din of the motorcycle. The moon shone high and bright now, so that the surrounding bush seemed to radiate a soft glow. When at last they reached the town, Jeevan surprised Joanna by driving past the turn-off to Momma Samuel's and continuing instead down the road to his own small shack. Joanna didn't protest but clung tighter to him. He pulled the bike into his dooryard and held it steady while she dismounted. He leaned the bike up against a tree, then placing his arm around her shoulder, he walked with her to the shack.

"Yuh must stay wid me de whole night," he said, his lips to her ear.

She didn't answer but took his hand from her shoulder and, holding it, led him toward the shack. At the steps she hesitated, thinking of Michael. If only he could see her now. She wondered if this was what he meant by other friends. She chuckled softly.

"Whad de joke, mahn?" Jeevan asked.

"Nothing," she said, then kissed him.

He took her in his arms and returned the kiss, his lips moist and open. She felt his tongue move in and out in search of hers through the gap between his teeth. Suddenly, she was tumbling into a deep, dark abyss. Her eyes shot open. She almost fell from his arms. She tried to hold him at arm's length. What was she doing? Too soon, she wanted to yell. But he tightened his grip around her, supporting her, drawing her closer to him. He kissed her face, her neck, her shoulders. She called out silently for Michael. But the vision that appeared was of Michael in another woman's arms, and a cold, determined hardness swept over Joanna, supporting her. She could do this. The strength returned to her legs, and she pressed her body into Jeevan's. He turned, took her hand, and stepped into the shack. Following him, she entered the darkness.

**

She woke the next morning to the sweet smell of marijuana. She could tell even before she opened her eyes that Jeevan was not in the lumpy bed next to her. Rising on an elbow, she looked to her left to see him, dressed, smoking a spliff at the kitchen table. He grinned and nodded. She saw her clothes in a heap on the floor. She clutched the sheet up to her neck and grabbed for her top. Why hadn't he stayed in bed until she had wakened, or better yet, wakened her with a touch? She would have liked to make love again this morning. She sighed, wishing he had managed a little romance. She dressed and went to sit across from him at the table. He offered her the joint. She shook her head. "Do you always smoke first thing in the morning?"

"Sure, mahn. Dis de second spleef Ah smoking. Ah smoke de first when Ah go and do me business first t'ing in de morning." His eyes danced.

"Your business?"

"Sure, mahn, Ah walk down to de shit-hole. Sit down wid me ganja and meditate on de trees." He smiled at her, gauging her reaction.

"Jeevan! I really don't need to know that." She reddened and looked out the window. They sat in silence while he finished the joint. He made no move toward Joanna but sat staring at her and smiling. He certainly wasn't acting like a smitten lover. She wouldn't mind a little snuggling right now. She considered going to sit on his lap. But there was something in his manner that made her hesitate. Probably he would find her foolish. She rubbed her nose and sneezed as the smoke from the spliff wafted across the table.

"Someone cheatin' on yuh," Jeevan said.

"What?" Joanna sneezed again.

"Sneezin' a sign dat somebody cheatin' on yuh." A smile flickered across Jeevan's face. "Maybe Michael?"

Her vision from last night, Michael in a woman's arms, flashed through her mind. Had she called out for Michael in her sleep? Was Jeevan trying to make her jealous? But how could she realistically be jealous of Michael now as she sat across from Jeevan after a night in his bed. Anyway, she was hungry, and it didn't look like Jeevan planned on offering her breakfast. She stood up so quickly she almost knocked her chair over. "Well, I guess I might as well go." She frowned when he nodded and said nothing. She took a few steps toward the door, but before she reached it, he bounded from his chair and stood blocking her way with his arm.

"When Ah must see yuh again?" he asked.

"Uh, I don't know," she said, confused by his hot and cold behavior. "When do you want to get together?"

"Yuh goin' today to de cliffs?"

She had been planning to spend the day at a cove where she

and Michael had spent some time. "Yeah, I thought I'd go out there."

"Ah check yuh dere," he said and let his arm drop so she could pass. Grinning at her, he said, "Yuh must stay away from de udder mahn, now."

She frowned. He really had a nerve. "We'll see," she said and moved past him down the steps.

***

They spent the next days in a whirlwind of ganja and sex, spending the hot nights together in Jeevan's single bed and separating in the morning just long enough for breakfast and a few errands. For Joanna, the days passed in a languid fog—a mix of long nights, broiling days, and too much ganja and beer. Jeevan's behavior towards Joanna flip-flopped between adolescent devotion and cool indifference. One minute he was fawning over her, and the next he was clipping his toenails. She chalked it up to the differences in their cultures and concentrated on enjoying the experience.

But, when she was alone, she often thought of Michael at work in his darkroom and wondered how he would feel about her escapade. She refused to think about what he might be doing in his off-hours. Thoughts of Michael often led to thoughts of Dave and whether he might return, but these, too, she pushed from her mind, unwilling to dwell on what she would do in that case. Now, there was Jeevan. Sometimes, it felt like there could actually be too many men in her life.

In the evening, Jeevan would pick her up at Momma Samuel's on his motorcycle, and off they would go to a local bar for drinking and dancing. Joanna felt as if she had left the tourist life behind and was immersed in the real Jamaica.

One morning, they separated as usual after waking. They made plans to meet up at a cove later that day. Now, Joanna lay alone on the beach, nestled between lush green growth on three sides, open to the sea on the fourth. She lounged on the soft, crystalline sand as gulls circled above, their laughing cries a counterpoint to the gentle breaking of the waves. The blinding sun moved behind a cloud, and Joanna sat up, glad for a few moments of shade. She wished she had a watch. What seemed like hours had passed with no Jeevan. As the afternoon dragged on, Joanna swung back and forth between rage and depression at the thought of being jilted. She waited by the water until the Jamaican sun drove her back to her house to nurse her pride and her sunburn. She was finishing dinner in the kitchen when she heard the roar of Jeevan's bike. She walked to the porch and folded her arms across her chest. Before he was even off the bike, she asked, "What happened today?"

Jeevan puckered his lips and looked at her.

"Where were you today?" Her voice sounded harsh to her own ears. A flock of crows flew overhead, their scolding caws echoing like an answer to her question. Joanna shaded her eyes and watched them pass. She needed to get control. He wasn't her boyfriend.

Jeevan climbed the steps, and sliding past Joanna, sat down on a chair, and propped his feet on the rail. "Why yuh ax a t'ing like dat?" he asked, his eyes dripping boredom.

His nonchalance bewildered Joanna. She shook her head and moved to sit on the railing. "Well, you were supposed to meet me at the cove," she said in a softer voice.

He leaned over and tied the lace on his sneaker. "Ah could no do so, mahn. Ah t'inking Dahlia soon come bahk."

"Dahlia!" Joanna stared at him, mouth gaping, eyes wide. "You told me she went back to her family!"

"Yeh, mahn." He looked at Joanna with a sheepish grin. "'Im say 'im soon come bahk before 'im go, and now 'im here."

"What! You knew she was coming back when we went to the beach that first day?"

He didn't answer right away but looked at the floor. Joanna thought about kicking him in the shin.

"Ah t'inkin' dat yuh be bahk in America before 'im comin' home," he said. "Ah feel dat 'im be visitin' 'im family ..." he shrugged, "maybe a mont'."

"But you just said she was coming back today?"

"Yeh, mahn. A friend 'im pass me de word."

Joanna collapsed into the chair next to him. She leaned her head back against the wall and closed her eyes. "Oh, Jeevan, that stinks. You should have told me! I never would have started with you if I thought she was coming back. I thought you guys were finished."

"No, mahn, 'im stick to me like mud 'cause Ah giving 'im money for food and a nice bed to rest 'im head."

They sat silent. Jeevan picked at his cuticles, occasionally lifting his hand and biting off a hangnail. Joanna tipped forward, elbows on knees, and rested her chin in her hands. Several of the children played out front. One young girl ventured toward Joanna.

"Yuh got any rubbish for me?" the girl asked. The kids had gotten used to collecting her trash for its treasures. Joanna smiled at her and shook her head. An insistent fly buzzed in front of the girl's face, and she brushed it away and scampered back to her playmates. Even as the sun was setting, the heat covered Joanna like a veil, and she longed for a cool breeze. She didn't really have the energy to fight with Jeevan. She sighed and turned to him. "You want a beer?" she asked. He nodded.

When she returned, two beers in hand, Wesley was leaning over the porch railing talking to Jeevan. Tension crackled between them, and they stopped arguing when she walked out and handed Jeevan the beer.

"Wesley tellin' me dat yuh been visitin' 'im," Jeevan said.

"Just once. I told you that," Joanna answered and sat down.

"Yes, man, just once," Wesley said, mouthing the words carefully and mimicking her accent. "And Ah come to check on yuh plenty times," he said with a sneer.

"Just a couple of times, Wesley." Joanna slouched in her chair and sipped on her beer, peering at Jeevan over the bottle.

He leaned forward and scrutinized Wesley through eyes narrowed to slits. "Hey, mahn, how can yuh go on so? Yuh must leave dis bodderation of de woman. Yuh makin' 'im plenty vexed."

Wesley turned his head and spat on the ground behind him. His face was blank, but the muscles in his neck stood out like ropes. "Yeh, mahn, Ah leave de place, now, but Ah soon come bahk." He shot a searing look at Joanna and disappeared around the side of the house.

Jeevan straightened up and leaned close to Joanna. "Where must we meet tonight?"

"Jeevan! I can't see you if Dahlia's back!"

"No, mahn?" He put on an innocent grin. "Why, mahn?"

"Jeevan! Because she's back. That's why."

He lowered his eyes to the floor and kicked at a bug. They both watched as the insect moved out of reach. "Okay, mahn. Den Ah check yuh tomorrow," he said, rising and vaulting the railing over to his bike. Joanna watched him guide the bike down the hill.

CHAPTER THIRTEEN

The sun beat down unmercifully. Joanna lay, hung-over, on a narrow strand of beach bordering a tiny cove. Jeevan had brought her here a few days ago. She hoped that the sun's heat might burn the alcohol's poison out of her veins.

"No tourist ever find dis place," he had assured her the day he showed her the cove. "Only Jamaican must know de way."

That day, they had ridden his motorcycle to a high cliff that jutted far out over the ocean. The straight drop had made Joanna dizzy as she peered over the edge to the water. To the side, a cave yawned in the gray rock of the cliff, its mouth open to the gentle currents of the ocean. Jeevan had hidden his bike in the high brush and taking Joanna's hand, led her to a path covered over with thick greenery. As they walked down the path, Jeevan yanked out great clumps of grass to clear the trail. Circling around through the dense undergrowth, they emerged onto a strip of pebbly sand, a child's secret place, nestled alongside a dense stand of sea grape trees. Joanna had found it magical.

But this morning, Joanna needed the long walk to the cove to sort out her jumbled thoughts. She had gotten very drunk after Jeevan left last night. She didn't smoke. She knew that would make her too crazy. By the time she staggered into bed, her thoughts of Jeevan and Michael and Dave had rolled themselves into one huge clump of rejection and guilt that weighed her down as if her heart had turned to lead and lay dead inside her. She was alone again, and her loneliness stretched like a dark tunnel before her. Unable to face the tourists at the other spots along the cliffs, she had taken the long walk to this secluded beach.

She reached into her backpack for her suntan oil. She eyed the trees bordering the beach, thinking they'd be a cooling retreat when the sun grew too strong. Only the dull murmur of the ocean lapping at the beach reached her where she lay although, for a moment, she thought she heard an airplane. She dismissed it and turned over on her stomach, prepared to get some serious rays on her back. She was dozing off under the warm blanket of the sun when a sound from the path in the brush startled her. It was Jeevan, loping toward her, grinning. Despite herself, she beamed at him. "Jeevan! What are you doing here?"

"Ah come to check yuh, mahn," he said. He sat down next to her on the sand.

"How'd you find me?"

"Ah searchin' all de places yuh like to swim. But Ah gettin' big surprise dat yuh walkin' all dis long, long way 'cause yuh strivin' hard so Ah doan find yuh." He laughed.

Joanna sat up and gazed across the beach to the ocean. "It wasn't just you. I didn't feel like seeing anybody."

They both stared into the clear, blue water of the cove. Off in the distance, a small fishing boat sailed along the coastline, the chugging of its little outboard barely loud enough to hear. Jeevan stood up and began to strip. He was down to his undershorts before Joanna could blurt out, "Jeevan, what the hell are you doing?"

"Goin' for a swim, mahn, goin' for a swim." He dashed off into the shallow water. Joanna watched him splashing in the gentle, rippling waves. "Sun hot," he called to her. "Ah feel yuh must come get cool." He waved his arm in a wide welcoming gesture. "Come, mahn," he shouted and splashed in the water.

She wrapped her arms around her knees. The sight of him, water dripping from his slim body was so tempting. She stood up, telling herself she was just going to get the sand off her legs although a part of her already knew she could end up over her head. Jeevan rushed in to meet her and, grabbing her around the knees, sent her tumbling backwards into the shallow water. "Jeevan!" She gave him a half-hearted scowl.

Before Joanna could move, Jeevan leaned over and kissed her, his body poised above her blotting out the sun. She pushed through his outstretched arm and jumped up from under him. The water swallowed her ankles as she looked down at him on his knees. "Jeevan, I can't do this. Not now that Dahlia is back. It's not right. I feel bad enough about before when I thought she left you."

"It doan matter, mahn. 'Im and me done done. Ah gonna send 'im back to 'im family, for true."

"Oh, God, Jeevan. Please don't do that. What about Christopher?"

"Doan matter. De womahn a bodderation. It got nu'tin' to do wid yuh."

She turned to wade out of the water, calling over her shoulder to him. "Doesn't matter. I still can't do this."

He huffed, bolted past her to the beach, and grabbed his clothes. He yanked them on, hopping toward the path, one leg in, one out. "No problem, mahn. Ah goin' for true," he yelled back at her.

***

After that day, Jeevan only came to the cottage during daylight, always on "business," to bring Joanna ganja or to change money for her. But she quickly discovered that from a certain place on the compound trail, she could see Jeevan's house and part of his backyard. Often, walking down the path on her way to the beach or in the evenings to High Hat's, she would catch a glimpse of Jeevan. Sometimes, she would see Dahlia at her chores. And, Dahlia, as if sensing that someone was watching, stopped her work, and stared up the hill, forcing Joanna to duck out of sight.

It was just two weeks since Michael had left, and she wrote to him almost every day, letters filled with her daily routine of shopping at the market, swimming by the cove, nights at High Hat's, descriptions of life at Momma Samuel's. She mentioned Jeevan often but always in his role as friend and provider, telling Michael of their trip to the beach on Independence Day and the dance in the hills. She knew Michael was no fool and might figure out about Jeevan.

She had gotten one letter from Michael, about a week after he left, hurriedly scribbled off to her, lamenting how busy he was and telling her to enjoy herself. He never asked about Dave, and to tell the truth, Joanna had almost forgotten about him herself.

One hot morning, Joanna gathered up her string bag ready to set out for the market. She took one long drag and squashed out the last of the spliff she had been smoking. As she stepped out on her porch, Jeevan appeared at her door. He was dressed in a ratty pair of pants and a shirt with the arms torn off, something she had glimpsed him wearing while he worked in the backyard. He looked as if some demon were nibbling at his insides. Joanna's knees shook. Something was obviously wrong. Had Dahlia found them out? It wouldn't be hard to do; every Jamaican for miles around had seen them together. She motioned Jeevan into the house and closed the door behind him. "What's the matter?"

"Dahlia say yuh must come right soon."

"Why? Why does she want to see me?" Joanna felt that familiar heart-thudding fear. This could only mean that Dahlia must know.

"Christopher sick," Jeevan said. "'Im say yuh must help."

Joanna took several deep breaths. "Help? How can I help?"

Jeevan shrugged. "'Im say yuh must come."

Joanna could barely swallow, her mouth was so dry. She licked her lips. What excuse could she possibly give? She wasn't sure that seeing Dahlia when she was high was such a good idea. But, somehow, she felt like she didn't have a choice. She gathered up her backpack. "Okay. I don't know what I can do, but let's go."

Jeevan stood, eyes downcast, kicking at a dust ball on the floor. "Ah canna do so, mahn. Ah must work some business."

"Jeevan!" Joanna almost dropped the backpack. "You have to come with me."

"No, mahn, Ah tendin' to business. Dere no danger dere. 'Im

not gone hurt yuh. Yuh must help wid de baby, dat's all." He continued to be intrigued by the dust ball at his feet, and she understood he wasn't going with her.

She was under no obligation to go, she told herself. It wasn't her fault the baby was ill, and there was nothing she could do. Yet, something gnawed inside her, a nagging feeling that her relationship with Jeevan somehow made her responsible. If he were simply her friend and not her lover, and Dahlia asked for help with the baby, wouldn't she go? "Okay," she said, as if issuing herself an order. She needed to go and face the firing squad, regardless. Throwing Jeevan a steely look, she marched out the door.

"Ah check yuh later," he said to her back.

**

Dahlia sat on a chair in their dooryard while the baby played in the dirt at her feet. Joanna propped her bike against a tree and hurried over to them. The baby looked up at her and cooed contentedly, but one cheek stuck out, grossly swollen with what looked like a monstrous, ugly boil. She knelt down and picked him up to look closely at his face. "Dahlia, what is it? Can he eat?" She worked to keep her voice from trembling.

"'Im eat, but 'im cheek blow up and grow plenty plenty hot." Dahlia reached over and placed Joanna's hand on the child's cheek. "Feel it. Hot."

"But how did that happen? Did a bug bite him? Did he eat something?"

Dahlia stared at Joanna for a long time without speaking, and Joanna felt as if she might wither under those scorching eyes if not from the heat of the fever in the baby's cheek.

"Yuh curse 'im on 'im name day," Dahlia said at last, spitting the words at Joanna.

Joanna's mouth dropped open, and she nearly lost her hold on Christopher. She put him down carefully and looked at Dahlia. "Dahlia. That's not true. I never meant any harm to come to him.

I didn't know the thing about his middle name."

"Someone must surely hear 'im name and curse 'im."

"Why would anyone want to do that? He's just a baby." Joanna felt like she might throw up. She steadied herself against the side of the shack.

"Many bad bad people in Jamaica," Dahlia said. And as Joanna watched, a veil descended over Dahlia's eyes. She began rocking in her chair to some beat only she could hear. "De spirits tellin' me de boy's fadder spillin' 'im fluids in anudder woman. Dey say dat mek de boy sick."

Dahlia seemed to rise slightly from the chair. The baby at her feet stopped his cooing to watch his mother. Joanna shook her head, trying to chase away the vision. A shimmering light spread out from Dahlia into the air, like hot air rising from a paved road in summer heat. Suddenly, Joanna felt a coldness, the dead chill of a dark, dank cave, drawing the heat from her body into Dahlia. She shivered and wrapped her arms around herself. The baby tilted his head to look again at Dahlia at the same instant that the veil seemed to lift from his mother's eyes as she glowered at Joanna.

Joanna felt sick as guilt welled up from the pit of her stomach. "Dahlia, what can I do," she asked, imploring the woman for relief from some nameless sorrow that froze every cell inside her.

"Yuh must give me de money. Den Ah takin' de baby to de doctor."

Dahlia's words fell like a warm cloak over Joanna. The chilling sorrow she had felt under the woman's terrifying look evaporated. Yes, this was something she could easily do. Joanna reached into her backpack and offered a handful of bills to the woman. "Of course, Dahlia. Of course. Here, take this money for the doctor. How much do you need?"

"Twenty dollah."

"Here, take it. I want to help. Really, I do, Dahlia. I never meant any harm." Her eyes moistened, and she looked away from Dahlia to the baby playing again in the dirt. She saw clearly that she was trying to buy off her guilt, but she couldn't help herself. "I never meant any harm."

***

Joanna didn't go to the cove that day. She walked instead to the spot near the cliffs where Michael and she had often gone, where she knew she would find other tourists. Thoughts of Michael and the familiarity of other Americans made her feel more secure, protected from the strange influence of the Jamaicans and the island. She kept to herself, nodding politely and smiling at the other sunbathers, then hiding herself in a book throughout the long afternoon.

That evening she only picked at Momma Samuel's dinner as she sat in the hot kitchen, avoiding the life of the compound visible from her front porch. When Momma Samuel came to take back the plate, she found it full. "My child," Momma Samuel said, "Yuh not well? Doan de food please yuh? Must Ah give yuh somet'ing else?"

"Oh, no, thank you, Momma Samuel," Joanna said. "I'm just not hungry tonight. Maybe it's the heat."

"De heat doan bodder yuh before dis," Momma Samuel said, looking at Joanna with a kind, motherly gaze. "Yuh must be missing yuh mahn, den. No?"

"Oh, yes, Momma Samuel. I'd be real happy if he were here with me right now." And Joanna meant it. She longed for the security Michael represented, longed to feel his arms around her, longed for just the sound of his voice to soothe her fears.

"Ah, yes, yes, child, Jamaica can be plenty plenty lonely place widout yuh mahn. But maybe yuh must learn to live widout him."

Joanna glanced up at Momma Samuel. The old woman's voice had changed, taking on a stern tone Joanna had only heard her use on her family. The wrinkles on her face deepened in the falling darkness of the kitchen, and she seemed to age as Joanna stared at her. Momma Samuel's eyes crinkled around the corners, her lips puckered into a small "o," and the skin of her

133

cheeks lengthened into jowls. Her vitality melted away from her until she looked like an old crone. And yet Joanna wasn't afraid.

"Why must I learn to live without him, Momma Samuel?" she asked.

The old woman leaned in toward Joanna and tilted her head to the side like a small bird listening for a far-off call. "Sometime, a woman get stronger widout 'im mahn," she said at last. "Yuh doan need no mahn to rescue yuh. Sometime, yuh must learn to bear yuh fear and live alone."

"Bear my fear? Like what?" But Joanna knew exactly what the old woman meant, for Momma Samuel had touched an exposed nerve. Joanna felt the familiar panic clutching at her stomach, her chest, her throat, constricting her every cell until she seemed to fold in on herself and become nothing more than a curled-up ball. That fear had chased her her entire life, stalking her, persuading her to do something, anything simply to escape it. The same fear that drove her to clutch at Michael, take up with Dave, and now Jeevan.

She looked at Momma Samuel, who studied Joanna. And in the midst of the fear that grabbed at her insides, a new thought snuck into her brain unbidden. Why the hell did she stay here? When things were going so well with Michael, after Dave vanished, why hadn't she gone home with him? To prove she could live without him? To him or herself? She didn't really know, but there had to be a reason. Her shoulders relaxed and dropped down, and the churning in her gut slowed.

Momma Samuel leaned over and placed the plate of food back on the table. She lifted the glass chimney from the lantern, and reaching into the pocket of her apron, she pulled out a single wooden match. Turning around, she struck the match on the rough surface of the wall behind her. Then cupping the flame in her hand, she lit the wick of the lantern, blew out the match, and looked at Joanna, her eyes searching Joanna's depths.

When Joanna didn't speak, the old woman pulled a chair next to her and sat down slowly, stiffly, her bones refusing to bend. She rubbed the knuckles on her right hand, each one a knot under her skin. She was no longer the sprightly, older woman Joanna had known for the last several weeks. Now, she bent as if she carried a heavy load on her back. She adjusted her weight in the chair and locked into Joanna's eyes until Joanna grew dizzy.

"Doan madder den why yuh stay," she said finally. Joanna jumped as the old woman answered her unasked question. "It just madder dat yuh here now. Dat so, because Jamaica 'ave a lesson to teach yuh, somet'ing yuh need learn, a lesson 'bout fear."

Somehow now, Joanna was not afraid. She knew what Momma Samuel said was true. Joanna didn't know how she knew. She just knew somewhere in the depths of her gut. Joanna floated above herself and looked down on the older woman. Joanna understood then that she had lived through this moment before with Momma Samuel. That perhaps she had lived through it many times. She was going to learn something extremely important at last, something she had been waiting for her whole life, or maybe even longer, something Momma Samuel would tell her. This was the moment. She sank back into her body. "What do you mean?" she whispered.

"Ah telling yuh dat yuh must be brave and live like death lookin' over yuh shoulder." Joanna sucked in her breath. Momma Samuel went on, "Ah sayin' yuh must never let fear rule yuh life lest death take yuh from behind when yuh runnin' in fear. No, my child, yuh must live life and do dos t'ings yuh love, so death only find yuh with joy in yuh heart." With this the old woman took Joanna's hand and laid it on Joanna's chest, and Joanna felt a warmth flowing into her like a burst of energy directed at her heart. "Den yuh 'ave no regret," said Momma Samuel, drawing her hand away from Joanna's. The warmth vanished, leaving an empty chill in its place. "But if death take yuh when yuh runnin' with fear," she went on, "den yuh spirit get trapped." Momma Samuel shook her head. "No, no, child, yuh must face yuh fear wid a brave heart."

"How do I do that?" Joanna asked.

The old woman shrugged and pushed her chair back to rise. She sprang up from the table, transformed once again into the agile Momma Samuel Joanna knew. And with a tender pat on Joanna's head, she left her alone in the tiny kitchen.

CHAPTER FOURTEEN

When Momma Samuel was gone, Joanna sat for a long time staring off into space. The lantern sputtered, snapping her out of her daze. She took a Red Stripe out of the cooler and walked through the house, checking the doors. In the bedroom, she closed the curtains despite the stifling heat and thought about the Jamaican woman's words. Yes, she wanted to live without the fear that had been chasing her forever. To live her life bravely. But how? It was all very well for Momma Samuel to tell her not to be afraid, but she had lived with fear so long that she had no idea how to go on without it. Her fear of being alone and unloved had morphed into a monster that overpowered and consumed her, so that every action she took was meant to escape that beast. How could she face it now?

As she sat in the sweltering little room, the strength she had felt under Momma Samuel's spell drained away, and the fear seeped in to fill the space. She went to draw back the curtain to let in some air but just as quickly yanked it shut to blot out the gaping darkness of the night. She thought of Dahlia that morning and the deadly coldness of the woman's eye. Dahlia had sucked all the heat out of her, leaving her with an ungodly chill. But was it Dahlia's spell or her own guilt that had chilled her? She shivered again in the suffocating heat. Whichever it was, she couldn't see Jeevan anymore, that much was clear. For the first time in days, she wished Dave would show up. Michael was too far away to help, but maybe Dave would come back to rescue her. She needed a man's protection. Maybe she should just go to Savanna-la-Mar and change her ticket for an earlier flight home.

She jumped at a soft knock on the bedroom door to the backyard. She stood paralyzed waiting for someone to burst through. A second knock, only this time louder. Was it Wesley?

"Joanna?" came a whisper through the door, then a shuffling in the gravel and her name again at the window. "Joanna?"

"Go away, Wesley," she hissed and looked for something to jam against the door.

"No, mahn. It Jeevan. Open de door. Ah must come in dere."

She stole to the window to peek out. Jeevan stood at the door now. "Joanna." He rattled the door handle. "Open de door."

She was so happy it wasn't Wesley, she rushed to open the bolt. At the sound, Jeevan shoved the door open. In an instant, she realized her mistake and cowered as far away from him as she could. Suppose someone saw him in her room? "Jeevan, I want you to leave me alone."

"Joanna, how yuh getting so crazy scared? It me, Jeevan, yuh friend. Ah come to tell yuh, Dahlia 'im took de baby to de doctor. 'Im give 'im de medicine. 'Im face, it already better, mahn. Cool down."

He sauntered over to the bed, plopped down, shaking the beer bottle off the dresser as he did. It clattered to the floor and shattered. Joanna stared at it as the last dregs of beer trickled onto the floor among the shards. Jeevan shrugged and grinned sheepishly.

Joanna disappeared into the kitchen and came back with a broom. Jeevan lunged from the bed and whisked the broom from her hands. She thought for a moment that he was actually going to clean up after himself, but instead he held the broom at arm's length away from Joanna. "Bad luck to sweep out de house after dark. Bring a bad bad stranger to yuh door."

"Give it back." She snatched the broom from him and swept the glass into a small trash basket then stood with the broom gripped tightly in front of her chest. "Jeevan, I told you. I don't want to see you anymore."

"Whad yuh talkin' so crazy, mahn?" He looked around the small bedroom. They had never been there together. "Where yuh stashin' yuh ganja, mahn?" he asked.

Without thinking, Joanna pointed to the dresser drawer. Jeevan leaned over and opened the drawer, rummaging around for the marijuana and papers. He rolled a spliff. "Ah feel yuh must sit down on de bed," he said. Joanna shook her head. "Come," he said and patted the bed next to him. "Yuh no gonna hit me wid dat broom." He laughed.

She set the broom against the wall and sat down, wrapping her arms tightly around her body. "Jeevan, she knows."

He licked the spliff closed. "'Im doan know nutt'in'. 'Im no see we in bed, for true. 'Im know nutt'in'." He held a match to the end of the joint, took several long drags, and handed it to Joanna. She pushed it back at him. "For true, mahn, dis will cool yuh down." Joanna took it and drew some timid puffs. "No, mahn. Smoke it," he commanded. She did.

"I know she knows about us, Jeevan. She just about told me this morning." Joanna had to make him believe her.

"No, mahn. Whad 'im say?"

"She said the spirits told her you were spilling your fluids in another woman."

Jeevan threw back his head and laughed until he began choking on the smoke. "No, mahn," he said between gasps. "'Im fishin'. 'Im hangin' de bait, seein' if de fish gone bite. 'Im doan know nutt'in'."

Joanna sprang from the bed and paced the tiny bedroom. "You're wrong, Jeevan. She knows."

"Come, sit down wid me," he said, offering her the spliff again. "When dis foolishness gone stop?"

She sat down, raising the spliff absently to her lips. He swatted at a mosquito nipping at his arm. "Yuh got Destroyer?" he asked.

She went to the kitchen, coming back with a coil in her hands. Setting it on the bureau, she lit it, then bent down to blow on the glowing tip until the curling smoke began to rise. As she lifted her head, the room swirled around her. She reached for the bureau to steady herself, but missed, nearly falling. Jeevan bounded up to catch her and set her on the bed. The room glowed a smoldering orange from the dim light of the lantern. He lifted it from the dresser and put it on the floor.

"Why'd you do that?" Joanna asked.

"It nice on de floor. It sexy, mahn."

She watched the light of the lamp as it flickered against the walls and ceiling. The fluttering quickened until it sputtered like a strobe. Her heart answered with its own rapid pounding. The very air, dense now with the smoke of ganja and punk, buzzed with the vibration of the light. A haze filled the bedroom, rounding its edges and corners, until it began to spin like a merry-go-round with her and Jeevan riding the outside. She grasped at the bed to stop the spinning.

Jeevan smiled at her. Joanna stared, suddenly captivated by the gap in his teeth. "Wesley will kill yuh, mahn," he said.

She watched him wide-eyed and shivered in the airless room. "What are you talking about?"

Jeevan shrugged. "Jamaican mahn get jealous, 'Im doin' crazy t'ings."

"Jeevan, stop it. You're scaring me." She crossed the room to the window, pulled the curtain back slightly, and peered out through a tiny gap. The backyard shimmered with a chilling blue-white glow. The reflection of the moon gleamed on the broad leaves of a banana tree. The shower stall, the garbage can, the bushes all stood out in eerie three-dimension like a slide in some giant ViewMaster. Each branch, each leaf jumped out in unnatural relief as she stared at the path that led to Wesley's. She tried to still her shaking hand and pulled the curtain shut again.

Jeevan smirked and tossed his stars and stripes cap onto the bed next to him, then settled back against a pillow. "'Im got a gun, yuh know."

"Shut up, Jeevan. I know he's got a gun." She grabbed his cap and jammed it back on his head. "Don't get too comfortable. Why are you telling me this?"

He pulled the cap down over his hair and eyed her closely. "Ah feelin' yuh doan wanna see me no more. Maybe yuh t'inkin' of takin' up wid Wesley."

She glowered over him. "Jeevan, don't be ridiculous. Dahlia's home. You're together, and there's no way I'm going to see you. I already feel bad enough about before. Don't you under ..." Joanna stopped mid-word and spun to face the window.

The gravel in the backyard crunched, and someone knocked at the back door. She looked at Jeevan, whose face mirrored her own shock. She took a step toward the door, but he reached out to grab her arm, shaking his head. She wrenched her arm loose from his grip but remained where she was. He motioned towards himself and shook his head again, then raised one finger to his lips for silence. "Who is it?" she called.

"It Wesley, mahn."

A dread descended on her like a black hood, and she tottered before a dark abyss. She glanced at Jeevan, who was smiling again at her. She called through the closed door, "What do you want, Wesley?"

"Ah come to beg some papers for spleef, mahn."

She stood motionless, trying to control the fear that roiled inside her like a hurricane. "I don't have any, Wesley," she said, her voice shaky, betraying her emotions. "Please go away. I'm very tired." She looked again at Jeevan, who nodded.

Wesley's voice shot like an arrow through the door. "Yeh, mahn, yuh very tired. Dat's for true. Yuh been runnin' 'round plenty plenty."

"Wesley, get out of here!" she shouted.

"Cool it, mahn. Ah gone."

They were silent, listening to the rustle of Wesley's footsteps retreating through the backyard into the bush. Soon only the hissing of the night insects sounded in the darkness outside. The familiar noises of the compound were quiet, the children long gone to bed, and even the dogs settled in for the night. As she listened, the insects' chatter grew into a shrill screech like a chorus of rusty screen doors. Joanna saw thousands of huge mandibles opening and closing, gnashing and chomping, coming closer, inching toward her back door. She flung her hands up to cover her ears. "Jeevan! What's that noise?"

"Whad noise, mahn?"

"The crickets. Why are they so loud?"

"It nutt'in', mahn. Just bugs. Sit down wid me and smoke some ganja."

"No," she screamed, clutching at his arm. "I want you out." She tried to drag him from the bed. "Now! I want you out, now!"

He stood up lazily, smiling. "Yeh, mahn. But Ah tellin' yuh, yuh must have some protection from Wesley. Doan Ah always watch out for yuh?"

"Out," she screamed again and darted to the door, grabbing the knob and flinging the door open. "Out," she said, pointing toward the darkness, her back to the open door. But the smile on Jeevan's face now twisted into a grimace. He jumped up, his eyes bulging, and stared past Joanna toward the door. She turned to look. "Dahlia!"

The big woman hurled herself through the door at Joanna, hollering like a raging bear. They fell onto the bed, Dahlia spitting out a string of curses, her bulky frame trapping Joanna beneath her. Joanna screamed for Dahlia to get up and tried to push the woman off, but she couldn't budge beneath Dahlia's weight. Jeevan rushed to the bed, grabbed Dahlia by the shoulders, and dragged her off. Joanna bolted through the open door and stood panting outside. She watched in horror as Jeevan grabbed Dahlia by the wrists, who kicked and screamed, struggling to free herself. Jeevan glanced at Joanna and shouted, "Run, mahn."

But she couldn't. Her legs were cemented to the ground. She searched behind her. Was Wesley watching, waiting with his gun? Crazed, she wrenched her eyes from the bush, back to the brawl in the room. Her thoughts ran wild. A love triangle! They'll kill each other, and she was in the middle. She had to get away from this insanity. She glanced around, frantic, desperate for a place to run, but what she saw only terrified her more. There, in the shadows, lay a dog, asleep, or dead, but totally unaware of the ruckus not four feet from its head. It was her dream of Reggae come to life in all its horror.

As Jeevan turned his head toward Joanna, Dahlia ripped her hands from his hold. She sprang through the door propelled by rage, landing next to Joanna with a force that almost knocked Joanna off her feet. But the jolt set Joanna free. She backed up, one step at a time with Dahlia matching her paces, their faces inches apart.

"Bomboclaat," Dahlia hissed. "White bitch! Why yuh come and mash up me life? Why yuh come and bring sickness on me baby? Why yuh try and steal me mahn? Why yuh no go bahk to 'Merica and live wid yuh own mahn? Whad yuh must say?"

Joanna's mind raced. What could she say?

Dahlia kept up her rant. "When Ah visit me family, me left eye ajump. Ah know someone talkin' 'bout me. Dey tell me dey see Jeevan dancin' wid a white woman."

Joanna spun around, desperate to outrun Dahlia's blistering tirade, but Dahlia followed close, screaming curses. "Go back to 'Merica, fancy lady. Leave Jeevan for me."

Joanna inched backwards, face-to-face with her accuser and raised her hands as if to protect herself from Dahlia's onslaught. "Jeevan and I are friends, Dahlia. You know that. He brings me ganja. I don't want him. I don't want to mess up your life. And remember, I'll be gone in a week. Things will be just like before. You've got Jeevan, and Christopher's better, right? I gave you money for Christopher, right?"

They came to the edge of the compound where the dark bush bordered the path to the ocean road. An unnatural silence fell on the night as if every ear in the dark compound listened intently to Dahlia's booming accusations. Far off, a lone dog howled, and an owl screeched in sympathy. The moon had fallen behind a bank of clouds, casting shadows along the ground like scurrying rats. Joanna shuddered. But still, Dahlia stalked her, the two of them caught in a terrible tango.

"Ah take yuh to de police," Dahlia said. "Give Babylon to Babylon. Ah tell dem yuh sleep in me bed and make a bodderation wid yuh rich ways. T'inkin' yuh do anyt'in' 'cause yuh rich 'Merican. Come here and mash up Jamaican life and go bahk home when yuh done. Bomboclaat! White bitch!"

Was it true? Had Joanna barged into their lives, uncaring of the harm she might do? She turned onto the ocean road. Roiling clouds smothered the light of the moon. The gentle ocean had turned angry, pounding the beach with its lashing waves. Lightning flashed far out over the water, then came the low rumble of answering thunder. But no rain fell into the murky black night. Joanna glanced over her shoulder. Should she try to rush past Dahlia back up to the relative safety of the compound? But, no. Wesley could be waiting for her, gun in hand. Yet every step with Dahlia took her farther down the dark road to High Hat's and away from any hope of safety. Whichever way she went, danger and horror lay waiting for her.

"Jamaica 'ave a lesson to teach yuh." Momma Samuel's words whispered in Joanna's ear as clearly as if the old woman were standing by her side. "A lesson 'bout fear. Don't let death find yuh wid fear in yuh heart. Yuh must be brave and turn 'round and face fear wid a strong heart."

Suddenly, Joanna understood there was no way she could outrun her fear. It was inside her, and she had to face it. She stopped so short that Dahlia bumped into her. The Jamaican looked dazed and backed off. "I'm going back," Joanna said. And as if Joanna's words were darts, Dahlia seemed to deflate before her eyes.

"Go, bitch," Dahlia said. "Leave de place." And without a backward glance, she turned toward the shack she shared with Jeevan, leaving Joanna stunned in the middle of the road.

Joanna had simply stood her ground, and Dahlia had quit, just turned around and walked away. It was too easy. It was a trap. Dahlia had lured her here to the inky road so Wesley could kill her. Joanna spun around and looked behind, her mind flooded with a dark, creeping dread. All her resolve shattered in the certainty that Wesley waited. She shivered so violently that her teeth chattered in the hot Jamaican night. She had dug her own cold, dank tomb. She wrapped her arms around herself and glanced at the road ahead and then behind her. He could be anywhere. Behind any bush, any tree. All the fears that had followed her forever rose again to blur into one huge tidal wave of terror. She was alone, without Michael, or Dave, or even Jeevan, facing Wesley's gun. There was no one to protect her.

"A lesson 'bout fear," came Momma Samuel's voice, again.

Joanna stopped shivering. Okay, get control, she told herself. If Wesley were out there waiting, what could she do about it? Nothing. She couldn't run to the police with her crazy story. She couldn't go back to Jeevan or anywhere else for that matter without walking the dark roads where Wesley could be hiding. There was no place for her to go. She could wait here in terror for Wesley, or, for once, she could not do something dumb simply out of fear.

She began climbing the hill to the compound. Her panic hovered just below the surface, ready to rise and choke her, but she clamped her mind shut on it, pushing the fear down. The moon slipped from under the clouds, lighting the path for a moment. She jumped, startled by the sudden shift, but forced her legs to keep walking, ordered them to move. She took deep breaths and kept her eyes glued to the road in front. If Wesley were hiding here, she would need to be ready to run. Maybe her screams would carry up the hill. She came to the path leading to the compound and followed it up. A stand of bushes brooded on either side. She willed herself to breathe slowly and stared straight ahead toward the dim glow where the bushes opened up. The moon ducked in and out of the clouds disorienting her as it played hide and seek. Her heart pummeled her chest with every step, but she had to get back to the cottage. As she approached the compound, the dogs took up their familiar yelping. She stopped short, realizing now that they had been silent throughout Dahlia's tirade. How could that be? Had Dahlia cast a spell on them, too?

She shuddered and hurried to the house. Once inside, she bolted the door behind her, circled the rooms, locking the front door and closing the windows. She crept into her bedroom where the lantern still flickered on the floor where Jeevan had set it. But all traces of him were gone. She went to the kitchen and dragged two chairs into the bedroom and propped them against each of the doors in the room. She collapsed on the bed, but soon the room was so hot that she had to open the sole window. Wesley would be able to see in to shoot her, but it didn't matter. She was suffocating. She needed to open the damn window.

She lay down again on the bed, leaving the lantern glowing, for she knew she wouldn't sleep. She tossed and turned all night, sometimes closing her eyes just for them to spring open a moment later. Only when the dawn broke did she manage to fall asleep, and then the voices of the children and the heat woke her soon enough.

CHAPTER FIFTEEN

Joanna changed her clothes and washed up but only nibbled at her breakfast. The events of the night played over and over in her head like scenes from some endless horror movie. Joanna saw again and again the image of Dahlia standing in the open doorway, the woman's face ghastly in the glow of the lantern, in that instant before they tumbled in a mass of arms and legs on the bed. That moment seemed somehow filled with meaning even now in the light of the morning. It couldn't be a coincidence that she had opened the door just then. Had Dahlia been listening? Had Wesley seen Jeevan go into the house? Or was it fate that had opened the door to the lesson Jamaica meant to teach her?

She sighed and ventured out to sit on the front porch to wait for Hosea, the ice man. She was counting out some change for him when she heard the rumble of a motorcycle turn onto the compound path. She dropped the remaining coins into his palm. He thanked her loudly and turned to leave just as Jeevan pulled up on his bike, nearly knocking Hosea over. The old man shuffled away, shaking his head.

Joanna stood at the steps, her hand on the post for support, her heart pounding, practically choking her with its pressure. How could he be so crazy, so reckless, to come up after last night? "Jeevan, what are you doing here?" she said, forcing the words through tight lips.

He balanced his bike against the side of the house and climbed the steps, brushing past her to sit on one of the chairs. He pulled up the extra chair and settled in, propping up one foot then the other, with exaggerated indifference. "Ah come to see if Ah must change some money for yuh today."

"Jeevan, I don't think it's smart for you to be here. Suppose Dahlia finds you here?"

"Fuck de bomboclaat," he said, his feet falling with a crash to the floor. "No woman tellin' me what me must be doin'!"

Joanna brushed the hair from her forehead and took a deep breath. "Listen, Jeevan, if you and Dahlia have problems to work out, please do me a favor, don't work them out over me." She turned from him to look down the path and back again. "Jeevan, I really want you to go."

"Yuh know, mahn," he said, suddenly a sulky little boy, "Ah just comin' here to do some business, dat's all. Yuh doan want to do no business wid me no more?"

Just a few days ago, Joanna had found the look endearing, but not now. "Jeevan, it's not that. You know that. It's just not smart, that's all. Dahlia's going to come up here and start making a scene again, and I can't deal with it."

He smashed his fist into his hand, making Joanna jump. "Ah mash up 'im face if 'im come givin' me vexation," he said.

"Jeevan! Stop that. I ..."

A commotion sounded from the bottom of the compound path. Joanna could hear dogs barking, children yelling and laughing, and when she looked, there was Dahlia storming up the path like the Pied Piper, Christopher in her arms and a trail of kids and dogs behind her.

"Oh, Jesus, here she comes!" Joanna retreated to the back of the porch as Jeevan jumped over the railing to lounge by his bike. He stood polishing his rearview mirror as Dahlia neared the porch. She stopped and planted her feet on the ground, shifting the baby from one hip to the other.

"Whad yuh want, womahn?" Jeevan asked in an ominous undertone.

"Ah want whad belong to me, yuh know," she answered, puffing up her chest in defiance.

"Whad must belong to yuh, now?" Jeevan huffed on the mirror and wiped it clean with the bottom of his shirt.

"Yuh must give me haf de furniture, and haf de dishes, and bed clothes and haf de money," she said as if reciting a speech. "Dat belong to me, and me takin' Christopher and goin' back to me family in de hills. Den yuh stay here wid dat bitch, and yuh screwin' 'im every day yuh want."

By now the crowd had grown to include most of the adults in the compound. Momma Samuel stood at the front of the group near the porch, scowling.

"Haf de furniture and haf de money?" Jeevan said. "Who buy dat furniture? Who makin' de money for dat furniture and dishes?" His voice stayed low and carefully controlled but rasped like the hiss of a lit fuse.

"Who livin' in dat house, and givin' yuh a son, and cookin' yuh de food, and washin'?" Dahlia said. "And all yuh doin' is makin' wickedness wid dat bitch and fuckin' in me bed."

Momma Samuel shooed away the children close to her and stepped between Dahlia and Jeevan. The crowd grew quiet. "Now hush," she said. "Yuh must stop makin' all dis fuss and such big ugliness in me dooryard. Yuh must go to yuh own house if yuh plannin' on carryin' on so." She pointed at Jeevan. "Ah doan ever see dis mahn come up here in de dark to look by dis 'Merican lady. Dere's no wickedness gone on in me house here." She took a step closer to Dahlia, dismissing her with a wave of her hand. "Yuh must go bahk home and take yuh vexation wid yuh."

Dahlia moved toward Jeevan and reached for his arm, balancing the baby on her hip. "Yuh must come bahk and give me haf of all de t'ings in dat house," she said.

Jeevan shook her off with such force that she almost lost her grip on the baby. She clutched Christopher as Jeevan pushed her back and swung his bike around toward the compound path. He jumped on the gas pedal and revved the bike, its exhaust roaring in Dahlia's face. Christopher cried out and hung on to his mother's neck as if to bury himself there.

Jeevan looked over his shoulder at Dahlia with a sneer so contorted that he was almost unrecognizable. "Ah show yuh haf de furniture," he said. "Ah show yuh whad belong to yuh." He gunned the bike and took off through the crowd, which opened like the Red Sea. As the roar of the bike faded, the people began to drift away to their homes.

Dahlia cast one more haughty look at Joanna and stomped away through the dust kicked up by Jeevan's exit. The Jamaican woman lumbered down the path, her head held high, baby on hip, as if still leading a procession. Joanna collapsed into a chair and rubbed her shoulders. She so wished Michael were there to massage them for her like he used to do when they were first together. She pictured him in the studio, sitting at the desk in front of the picture window, probably on his third cup of coffee. She sighed. He was so far away, in another world, a safe world. She stood up, thinking she should ride down to the market for some food, but her heart was still throbbing in her throat, and she felt empty as if Dahlia had stolen her last bit of energy … again.

As Joanna sat staring blankly around her, a group of the children began running, chattering, and pointing toward the path to the road. She leaned over the porch railing and saw a crowd forming near the crest of the path. Some people were pointing over the trees while others stood on their toes, straining to see something. She edged toward the crowd, which buzzed and bubbled with tension. As she approached the group, she heard snatches of conversation.

"De boy's crazy.... takin' out de furniture... mashin' up ..."

Horrified, Joanna realized the crowd was standing on the spot that looked down onto Jeevan's yard and house. She stumbled as the blood drained from her head and reached out to lean against a small palm tree. Some of the people had turned to look at her and were shaking their heads. She wanted to run and hide, but she needed to know what Jeevan was doing.

Suddenly, the crowd's murmuring went up an octave. People jostled each other aside to get a better view. One little girl jumped piggy-back onto an older man to peer over his head. A woman turned to Joanna and hollered, "De boy pourin' kerosene!"

Then, as if one person, the crowd gasped, and people began shouting and screaming. Joanna saw a wisp, then billows of dark, black smoke rising into the sky above the trees like puffs from some gigantic spliff. "Oh, no," she whispered.

A woman came running from the crowd. The sleeves of her checkered house dress fluttered as she ran towards Joanna. "'Im setting all de furniture afire!" she said gasping, with a look of pity that Joanna didn't understand. "'Im drag all de t'ings out de house. Den 'im take a ax and mash dem up. Den 'im pour on de kerosene and ..." The woman threw her arms in the air. "Poof! Arson! De police must surely come and take de boy away. Arson big big crime now. Dey 'fraid for revolution."

Joanna stared horrified as smoke filled the air and soot particles floated to the ground. More of the crowd had turned to face her, shaking their heads. She stared at them. She wanted to tell them it wasn't her fault. It couldn't be. She hadn't done anything horrible, hadn't meant to break up a family. Why was he burning the furniture? Why was he doing such a stupid thing? Why couldn't he just give Dahlia half the stuff. What was the big deal? He was crazy. She brushed soot from her face. The sockets around her eyes ached with the tears she held back.

Another roar went through the crowd like a blast of air coming to bowl Joanna over. What was he doing? Was he hurting Dahlia? Or the baby? Should she do something?

"Police ... police ... take de boy ... tie 'im hands."

The ground seemed to sway beneath Joanna. Her legs wobbled. She had to sit down. She put both hands against the palm for support. Her head swam. She needed her visor. She had come out without her visor. How stupid! If the police were involved, if they arrested him, they would find out he was selling weed, changing money. Would they come to arrest her for buying weed from him? For dealing on the black market? Oh, God, she needed Michael.

The crowd began to disperse. Two little girls came skipping up to Joanna. "De policemahn take de boy to jail," began one, her eyes wild with excitement.

"Did you see them take him away?" Joanna asked. Both children nodded solemnly, then ran hand-in-hand back towards Momma Samuel's kitchen shack.

Other people passed her, glancing at Joanna, gesturing, and talking among themselves. An elderly man stopped in front of her. He took his cap off and wiped his forehead with a red bandana. "Dat boy plenty plenty crazy," he said and walked away, shaking his head.

When everyone was gone from the path, Joanna slunk over to where the crowd had stood. She balanced on her toes to see into Jeevan's yard. A large pile of black boards still smoldered like the charred remains of some roasted animal. Dahlia and Christopher were nowhere to be seen. As far as Joanna could tell, the structure of the house was undamaged. Perhaps Dahlia was inside. Had he burned all the furniture? Where would Dahlia and the baby sleep tonight?

She sank to the ground like a rag doll, her head in her hands on her bent knees. Images of Dahlia and Jeevan mixed with the grey smoke in her mind, and scenes from a Jamaican movie played before her eyes. She saw the jailer dragging Jeevan into the center of a courtyard, tying him hand and foot over a barrel, pulling back with an ugly switch in his massive hand ... and then the scene blurred. She shook her head. Was it really her fault? True, they might be crazy. But, still the guilt swamped her, and she felt like she might vomit. This never would have happened if she hadn't gotten involved with Jeevan. Hadn't she been the one to light the match? She looked up and saw Momma Samuel striding toward her. She waited, miserable, for the woman to accuse her.

"Come," the old woman said, standing over Joanna's hunched figure. "Come." She put her hand under Joanna's arm and pulled her gently up. "Yuh must come bahk de house and eat yuh food. Ah mek some nice sam'wich for yuh. Dat boy and dat girl long-time plenty plenty loco," she said. "Dey fight all over de town. Don't vex yuh mind no more wid dem."

Joanna nodded and followed Momma Samuel up the path.

***

Joanna spent the rest of the day in the compound. She sat on the porch, her brow knitted, chewing on her nails, and considered her situation. It was hot. The sweat beaded on her forehead and upper lip and ran down her chest. Maybe she should venture out to the ocean or go find some Americans. But she winced at the thought of walking through town. She dreaded the accusing stares of the Jamaicans. Surely by now, the whole town would know what had happened and about her part in the sordid thing. She imagined the road lined with people pointing at her. And suppose she saw Wesley or Dahlia? She hoped she'd never see either of them again. Instead, she sat on the porch, brooding on the horrible mess, her thoughts skittering around like a flock of Momma Samuel's chickens.

She had had enough of Jamaica. She wanted to go home. Tomorrow, she would go to Savanna-la-Mar, change her ticket for an earlier flight, and get the hell out. Yes, it was horrible that Jeevan was in jail, but what could she do? She certainly wasn't about to go to the police herself to bail him out. They'd probably arrest her. Or maybe they didn't even have bail in Jamaica. No, there was nothing for her to do but leave.

Besides, it wasn't really her fault anyway. Hadn't Jeevan brought the situation on himself with his obnoxious macho attitude and his stupidity in burning the furniture? And was Dahlia any better with her greedy, manipulative ways? Their relationship had been in trouble well before Joanna had gotten involved with Jeevan. If it hadn't been Joanna, it would have been another woman. But, then, what would become of Dahlia and Christopher if Jeevan stayed in jail? How would they live? Where could they stay?

She bounded from her chair and strode back into the house to her bedroom. She dragged her suitcase from underneath the bed and began pulling clothes from the bureau drawers. She was folding a cotton top into the suitcase when she thought she heard a timid knock on the front door. It must be one of the children, she thought. "Who's there."

After a moment, the answer. "It Dahlia."

Joanna froze, hand in mid-air, blouse suspended above the suitcase. The sweat on her neck turned to ice, and she thought of running out the back door. But no, she would not run this time. Where could she run anyway? She dropped the blouse on the bed and, bracing herself, walked through the cottage to the front door. Dahlia stood, Christopher on hip, on the other side of the screen door. Joanna opened the door and stepped outside before Dahlia could maneuver her way in. "What do you want, Dahlia?" she said, flint in her voice.

Dahlia lowered her eyes to the floor and didn't speak for what seemed like a long time. At last, she raised her eyes to meet Joanna's and smiled sadly. "Ah come to beg yuh help."

Joanna tensed. The woman was going to try and get more money out of her.

"How me and de child must live if Jeevan in jail? How Ah must get money to feed de child? Ah doan even 'ave de money to go bahk to me family in de hills. How Ah must find a way home?"

Joanna folded her arms over her chest. She swallowed hard and tightened her gut against the rising bile and the woman. She would not give Dahlia any more money.

A heavy silence fell between the two women as Dahlia stared at the floor. The baby in her arms squirmed and reached towards Joanna's shiny earring. Joanna took his chubby little arm in her hand to keep him from pulling on her ear and felt a rush of compassion like a wash of warm water melting the ice in her gut. What about Christopher? Certainly, he was innocent. Could she deny him help when it was she who had, if not caused, at least played a part in landing his father in jail?

Dahlia reached out to pull the baby's arm to his side, then spoke again, her eyes still on the floor. "Yuh must give me money for attorney to free Jeevan," she said. "Den 'im be able to take care of me and de baby."

Dahlia looked up, and Joanna saw a hard glint return to the

woman's eyes. Joanna shivered, feeling that chill again. But Joanna knew that Dahlia had no intention of hiring a lawyer for Jeevan. She would use the money for herself and the child, leaving Jeevan to languish in jail. But, wasn't that what Joanna had been intending to do only moments ago? Still, something inside her balked at handing over the money.

"Can an attorney get him out of jail?" Joanna asked.

Dahlia nodded.

"How much would he need?"

"Maybe one hundred dollah 'Merican."

Joanna did a quick calculation. All she had left was a hundred-dollar traveler's check and sixty dollars Jamaican from the last one Jeevan had changed for her. If she went to Savanna-la-Mar, she could call Michael from the phone in town to wire her more money. It would be worth a hundred dollars, she realized, just to soothe her conscience and get Jeevan out of jail. But she would not give the money to Dahlia. She looked the woman square in the eye. "I'll go to Savanna-la-Mar tomorrow and hire the lawyer myself. I have to go anyway to change my ticket. I've decided to go home as soon as possible."

Dahlia's eyes bored into Joanna. Joanna's heart thudded in her chest, but she met the woman's stare without wavering.

"Isn't that what you wanted, Dahlia? Didn't you want to hire a lawyer for Jeevan? This way you won't have to go to Savanna-la-Mar yourself."

Dahlia's face seemed to grow flush under her dark skin as her lips set into a tight knot. Christopher abruptly quit his soft chattering. He turned in Dahlia's arms to watch his mother and began to whimper. Joanna wanted to reach out to comfort him but was afraid.

"And how Ah must feed dis littel child dis night, missus 'Merican lady, now dat 'im fadder in jail?" Dahlia spit the words at Joanna with such force that Joanna gasped for breath as the spray of Dahlia's saliva hit her in the face.

"Dahlia. I only have sixty dollars Jamaican on me," Joanna said and realized instantly that the sum must seem like millions to the Jamaican woman. Embarrassed, she stammered, "I ... I can give you twenty," and turned back into the house quickly to find her wallet.

"Bomboclaat," Dahlia yelled at her back, but Joanna ignored the curse and returned with the money in hand.

"Here, Dahlia, that's all I can give you."

The woman snatched the bill from Joanna's hand and shoved it roughly into her bosom. The air around Dahlia began to flicker and seemed to spread like a suffocating cloud toward Joanna. Joanna gasped for breath.

Dahlia began to speak, her voice low and measured. "For true, Ah feel someday yuh will grieve for what yuh done wid yuh rich lady ways. Yuh will suffer like Ah suffer. Den maybe dat day yuh be sorry." Turning abruptly, she stomped off the porch.

Joanna stood watching as Dahlia swayed regally down the path, disappearing around the curve in the road. But even when Dahlia was out of sight, Joanna could still feel the chill of the woman and her words. Something caught at the corner of her vision, and she turned quickly to see a large moth flitting by her head. A moth in the daytime? Despite the strong light of the morning sun, flickering shadows seemed to fall all around her like the dappling of fluttering leaves in a strong summer breeze. She sank down, thinking she was about to faint, until the wavering spots faded. As if in a slow-motion movie, the sights and sounds of the compound seeped back into her mind. The children played a game of tag, darting in and out between the flimsy shacks and underneath the line where Momma Samuel stood hanging wash. The older woman shooed them away as they scurried among the wet clothes. Joanna wondered if they had all been there throughout her exchange with Dahlia. As if in response to her thoughts, Momma Samuel placed the last of her clothes on the line and came over to stand before Joanna.

"Dis woman try to work evil spirits on yuh," she began. She swatted away the moth that still darted around Joanna's head. "See? Dat moth mean a duppy 'round."

Joanna drew a sharp breath. "A duppy?"

"Yes, missy, a ghost." Momma Samuel held up her hand for silence and went on. "Yuh must fight 'im and de fear inside yuh. Yuh must face dem and walk t'ru de spirits and not run from dem. Yuh must show death dat yuh do not hide in fear but walk in de light."

Joanna began to shake. She was totally exposed, totally vulnerable. The air, the clouds, the protecting sky were all at once gone, and the cold, dark void of space reached down and touched her with its icy fingers, as if someone had snatched a warm cap from her head in the middle of a blizzard. The energy of the cold, indifferent universe streamed down from above directly into her skull, smothering her in its nothingness. She flung her hands to her head to shield herself from the deluge but that offered no protection. She looked up to see Momma Samuel's clear eyes staring gently at her. "But why?" Joanna said, feeling as if her whole life rested on Momma Samuel's answer. "Why is this happening to me?"

The old woman shrugged. "Dis de way of life. Dis de lesson from de stars and heavens above." She reached out to pull Joanna's hands from her head. "Dere, now. Soon come, Ah bring yuh de dinner. Yuh must eat and build up de strength for yuh journey home." She smiled and ambled back to her cooking shed, leaving Joanna to consider her words.

CHAPTER SIXTEEN

Joanna somehow managed to reach the round-about at the center of town although she remembered little except for the stomach-churning fear that had accompanied her every inch of the way. But, despite that, she steeled herself and kept walking. She avoided the eyes of passers-by and stared straight ahead. Someone called out to her as she passed. It was the woman who had sold her banana bread on the way to Savanna-la-Mar, "For true, de boy, 'im in plenty plenty big trouble, now." She nodded but kept walking.

She was very tired. She had been up most of the night forcing herself to read to stay awake, the lantern burning by her bed to scare off the same shadows that followed her even now. Darting forms chased her as she walked, vanishing just as she turned to face them. Were they evil spirits, ghosts, as Momma Samuel had said, or simply her own creations? It didn't matter, she had to do what she had set out to do despite her fears.

Those fears had been real enough to keep her from sleeping all night. Only when the dawn began to seep into her room, did she finally blow out the lantern and lay down to sleep. She awoke several hours later, soaked in her own perspiration. She downed two cups of coffee and managed a few dry bits of toast that clung to her throat like sand. Then she quickly donned a skirt and t-shirt and set out for the bus stop.

Now, she sat on a small clump of rocks by the side of the road under the hot sun. Despite her visor and sunglasses, the glare of the light set a small hammer pounding in her head. After the long walk on so little sleep and even less food, the sun was making her woozy. She looked around, searching for a shady spot. But only the bare, dusty road greeted her.

She concentrated on the spot in the road where the bus would appear. A sudden motion caught her eye. She swiveled to look but saw only the wavy shimmer of the heat rising from the dirt. Then, something flitted so close to her face she could feel the quiver of its wings on her skin. Yelping, she jumped up and batted at her head. A moth! She hopped up and down, waving her arms and hollering, then stumbled as the blood drained from her head. She plopped awkwardly to the ground, her legs splayed before her in the dirt. Glittering flashes burst like tiny stars in the air before her, and she lowered her head between her outstretched legs. Slowly the blood returned to her head, and the strange sensations faded. She looked around and saw her sunglasses in the middle of the road where she had flung them in her panic. She rose cautiously, dusted off her skirt, and went to fetch them. She retreated to her seat on the rocks, sneaking glances to all sides to see if anyone had seen her insane performance.

If she kept this up, they might just come to take her away. She managed a humorless chuckle. But it was clear that, whether the things following her were Dahlia's evil spirits or only bugs, she had to keep hold of herself. She had been running so long like a hysterical child from every real and imagined danger. Running to Michael, to Dave, to Jeevan. Running from Wesley, and Dahlia. Running from her fears. Running from herself. Each step she had taken since coming to Jamaica—or maybe even through her whole life—had led her racing wildly to this very spot, to this very moment. She had to stop now, or she would find herself so far from her path, literally and figuratively, that she might never get home again.

She looked up to see the bus rolling down the road. She collected her backpack. She just had to keep it together a little longer, and soon she would be safe.

***

The bus stopped in front of the courthouse. Joanna jumped down, relieved to breathe fresh air at last after the stench of hot, sweaty bodies, live chickens, dead fish, all muddled up like a mix of dirty socks and day-old garbage.

A lithe young woman chatted on the pay phone outside the courthouse. She whispered into the mouthpiece, cupping it in both hands as if caressing it. Joanna waited nearby, trying not to stare impatiently as the woman cast disdainful glances at her. The last bus left for Negril at three. That left Joanna four hours to do what she had to do in town.

Joanna fidgeted with the coins for the phone, her eyes darting here and there. Was it only a few weeks ago that she had been here with Michael and Dave? Then she had been exhilarated by the wonderful mix of unfamiliar people, sights, colors, smells. Now she saw only an alien, menacing blur on every side.

The woman on the phone reached into her straw purse and dropped another coin in the slot, glaring at Joanna, as if daring her to say something. Instead, Joanna wandered over to the courthouse steps and sat down. The last thing she wanted was another confrontation with a Jamaican woman. At last, the woman hung up the phone and, throwing Joanna one more reproachful look, marched away.

Joanna hurried over to the phone and thumbed through the phonebook dangling from the stand. She ran her finger down the list and found the number quickly, then dialed the airline in Montego Bay. The clerk said she could easily exchange her ticket although he couldn't change the booking over the phone. There were several flights a day to the U.S., he said, but she would have to come to the airport and take her chances. She hung up. She had hoped she could arrange it all by phone, but it would have to do.

She tapped the switch again and dialed the operator who informed her that all the lines to the mainland were busy. Joanna could leave her number and wait for a line to open up. She slammed the receiver down and leaned her head against the side of the phonebooth. How many more roadblocks would she have to face? Joanna stood by the phone, her hand on the lifeless receiver, praying that no one would come to use it. She held the phone to her ear and pushed the cradle down so anyone near would think that she was actually talking. She kept up a mumbled dialogue with herself to maintain the illusion. She was not giving up this phone. At last, it rang.

"We 'ave a line to the mainland, ma'am," the operator said and asked Joanna for the number.

As the phone rang, Joanna let out a deep breath, as if a band around her chest had loosened. The line clicked, and Joanna heard the familiar voice of one of the women on Michael's answering service.

"Will you accept a collect call from Joanna in Jamaica?" the operator asked.

"From Jamaica?"

"Yes, ma'am. Joanna is calling from Jamaica."

"I can't accept a call from Jamaica," the woman answered, clearly impatient.

Joanna was stunned. She stammered, "It's ... it's Joanna. ... It's an emergency!"

"They won't accept the call," the operator said.

"It's Michael's girlfriend Joanna. How many times a day do I talk to you? I know you recognize my voice. I'm in Jamaica, and it's an emergency!"

There was a buzzing, then a slight crackling. "I'm sorry, I can't accept a call from Jamaica."

"Fine. Just forget it, operator," Joanna yelled into the phone. "I want to make another call." She gave her mother's number but got no answer. "I have another one, operator," she said, giving Michael's mother's number. The phone rang. Joanna's heart beat so fiercely that it pounded like a bass drum in her ears. Still the phone rang. This wasn't possible. What was happening? Why couldn't she reach anybody?

"They're not answering," the operator said. "Please try again later."

"Wait," Joanna shouted. "I know they'll answer soon."

"I'm sorry. That's twelve rings. I'll 'ave to disconnect."

The dial tone buzzed like an angry gnat in Joanna's ear. She moved the phone from her ear and stared at it, a dead thing in her hand. She had never felt so completely alone in her life. Cut-off entirely by an ocean from every person she loved and trusted, from anyone who could possibly help her. She sighed and glanced at the clock atop the courthouse. She was wasting time. She would find the lawyer first, then come back and try again. Slinging her backpack onto her shoulder, she strode toward the doors of the courthouse.

Once inside, she quickly found the reception desk at the end of a long, marble-lined hall. The clerk looked up languidly from the papers he was reading as she asked for the names of some lawyers in town. He wore a long-sleeved white shirt, the sleeves rolled up to his elbows, a plastic visor on his head like some card dealer at a casino. Smirking, he asked, "Your boyfriend get busted for drugs?"

Joanna shook her head and explained that she had a Jamaican friend who had gotten in trouble for burning some furniture. The clerk nodded, but the smile continued to flicker on his lips. "Arson," he said. "That big crime in Jamaica these days. I know the lawyer for your friend." He opened the desk drawer at his waist, pulled out a tattered business card and handed it to Joanna. "This man will help you. His office right down the street."

Joanna thanked him and left the courthouse, glad to be away from him and in the air again. Once on the street, she looked at the card: William Gray, Esquire, and an address. She walked past a few shops, searching for street numbers, but found none. She noticed a woman approaching, and taking a deep breath, went to speak with her. The woman directed Joanna to a seedy-looking building two blocks away, a two-story stucco structure with two large ground-floor windows covered with sheets of corrugated metal. A double door between the shuttered windows swung open as Joanna stood hesitating on the sidewalk, and a man walked out. Joanna moved toward him and showed him the business card. "Is this the office of William Gray?"

"Sure, mahn."

"Is he any good?"

The man shrugged and sauntered away.

Joanna swallowed, brushed her hair off her face, and entered the building where she found herself in a small room. A number of Jamaicans sat on benches along the walls, and Joanna reddened as every face turned toward her. For a moment, she wondered if news of Jeevan's escapades had traveled all the way to Savanna-la-Mar. She ran her hand nervously through her hair and looked around for a place to sit. An older woman, fanning herself with a magazine, moved over, making room for Joanna. Joanna thanked her and took a seat.

"Is the lawyer in?" she asked the woman.

"Yes, missy. 'Im talkin' wid a mahn, now, yuh know."

"Do you have to have an appointment?"

"No, no appointment." The woman put her hand on Joanna's arm. "Yuh must just wait yuh turn, dear."

Joanna smiled, nodded, and counted five people ahead of her. She might never get in at this rate and wondered if this was the only lawyer in town. The heat plus the smell of sweaty bodies threatened to bring up what little food Joanna had eaten. "Hot in here," she said to the woman and moved closer to the windows that opened onto an alleyway. Although she doubted she could concentrate, she rummaged in her pack for a book and forced herself to read. A door into the room opened and out walked a large, pale-skinned Jamaican man. He looked about fifty, his light blue shirt opened at the neck and soaked with perspiration under the arms and down the front. He yanked a handkerchief from his pants pocket and wiped his forehead. An old man with a cane limped behind the lawyer.

"Now, you do what I told you, and don't worry," the lawyer said, guiding the man towards the door. "I'll send you the papers in the post."

When the old man was gone, the lawyer came over to Joanna. "Someone in trouble with drugs?" he asked, smiling. His smug certainty echoed the courthouse clerk's grating attitude. She kept her face blank and explained she had a Jamaican friend in jail. The lawyer raised an eyebrow. "Well, you'll have to wait your turn, miss," he snapped, as if Joanna had asked him to take her out of turn. He turned his back to her. "Next," he called.

She watched out the window as the shadows marched across the dirt alleyway. There were still four people in front of her, so when the door to the office opened again, she stood up. "Excuse me. Can you tell me what time it is, please?"

"I don't wear a watch," Gray said. "Don't worry. I'll get to you."

"It's just that I have to make the bus to Negril at three."

"I said I'll get to you. You'll make your bus." He ushered the next client into his office.

The woman with the fan spoke. "Yuh be able to see de clock on de courthouse from de udder side of de road, yuh know. But Ah feelin' it nowhere close to t'ree, now."

Joanna swallowed hard. Her mouth was so dry, she had trouble speaking. "Thank you," she managed to get out.

"'Mericans every day worried 'bout de time," said a young man sitting on the bench across from the window. "Dey always sooo busy," he muttered. His words shot at Joanna like darts.

She went outside and crossed the street. The courthouse clock said one o'clock. Should she go make the call to Michael now and forget about seeing the lawyer? But what about Jeevan? She couldn't really just let him rot in jail. And besides, she had told Dahlia she would hire a lawyer. If she didn't, she would have to give Dahlia the money, and what good would that do Jeevan? But either way, she would only have forty dollars left.

Her mind filled with a flood of fears, threatening to drown her. If she couldn't reach Michael, would she have enough money to get to Montego Bay? What if a war started, and Jamaica were cut off from the rest of the world? And all the phones went dead? Suppose she got trapped forever in Jamaica, broke, at the mercy of the Jamaicans? She shook her head, no, and squared her shoulders. She had to stop this. She was making herself crazy as usual, and besides, hadn't she learned the lesson yet? The lesson on that dark road? Dahlia had simply turned around when Joanna had the guts to face her. And then she had had the strength to walk the road that night even as fear of Wesley tore at her throat. If she could face that, she could face this.

She crossed the street and stepped back into the building. The woman with the fan smiled at her. Joanna walked over to sit by the window again, hoping for a breeze. Outside, a goat nibbled at garbage from an overturned can. She turned away, repulsed by the squalor, as the door to the office opened once more. The young man who had taunted her hurried through the foyer and out to the street. The lawyer beckoned to the woman with the fan, but she pointed to Joanna. "Yuh must go in, missy," she said. "Ah got all de day long, for true."

Joanna thanked her and glanced at Gray. He nodded, and Joanna followed him into his office. A noisy floor fan blew hot air around the small room. He sat down heavily behind a massive wooden desk, piled high with papers and manila folders. Several large cabinets lined the walls, their open drawers bulging with files. More stacks of files and newspapers were strewn on the floor, with no space in the office free of clutter. Joanna wondered how he could possibly find anything. Her heart sank, and her confidence wavered.

He tipped back in his chair and lit a fat cigar. His hair lay flat on his head, as if slicked down with grease. His fleshy face and neck gleamed, too, with oily perspiration. He reminded Joanna of a TV wrestler greased up for a match. Puffing deeply, he watched Joanna through heavy-lidded eyes. She looked away, unsettled by his creepy gaze.

Finally, he said, "So tell me, little lady, what's the problem?"

"I've been staying in Negril ..." she began.

"With the hippies," he said, scoffing.

"No, not with the hippies. With my boyfriend." Above the whirl of the fan, Joanna heard what sounded like a goat bleating below the open window. She jumped.

Gray laughed, clearly amused by her discomfort. "It's just a goat. A little native fauna." He smiled and narrowed his eyes.

"And where, might I ask, is your boyfriend?"

Joanna rubbed at a spot on her skirt and avoided his eyes. "He had to go home on business."

Gray raised one eyebrow and pointed at Joanna with steepled fingers. "And left you all alone? What a dangerous thing to do."

Joanna ignored his implication and went on. "A Jamaican friend of mine had some trouble with his wife. They got into a big fight, and he got pretty crazy and burned all the furniture in his house."

"Arson! That's very serious, you know. We've been having some problems with arsonists. Revolutionaries, they call themselves. Our parliament recently passed a hard new law against arson." He studied Joanna. "Your friend could end up in jail for a long time." He exhaled a cloud of cigar smoke squarely in Joanna's direction and leaned in toward her. "And did you have anything to do with the trouble your friend had with his wife?"

Joanna felt her stomach flip at his intimate tone. If he tried to touch her, she would vomit. "I don't see what that has to do with anything," she said. "I'm simply here to get some help for my friend."

"Yes, I see." He straightened up and moved a few papers around on his desk, all business again. "Then, what can I do for you?"

"I want to hire you to defend him, get him out of jail."

He pursed his lips and crossed his arms atop his ample stomach. "You want to hire me? Can you pay my fee?"

"Well, it depends on how much it is."

"How much do you have?" he said, locking his gaze on her.

She hesitated and bit her lip. "Not much. I ... I need some money to get home. I could give you a hundred dollars."

He smiled broadly. "That's fine. I can take the case for a hundred American."

The moment he agreed, Joanna knew she had been had. What Jamaican would ever have a hundred dollars to pay him? But it was done, and, at least, it would relieve her guilt and leave her a little cash until she could get money from Michael. If he wired it today, she could pick it up at the post office in Negril.

"You give me the hundred dollars, and I'll get your boy out of jail before too long," he said and shoved some papers into the desk drawer.

She reached into her pack for her wallet. "Will you take traveler's checks?"

He laughed. "I'll take anything." His belly jiggled underneath his shirt.

She signed the five checks and handed them to him, then wrote down Jeevan's name and "from Negril." She stood up and moved toward the door. He sprang from his chair and intercepted her, putting his arm around her shoulder. She felt the warm wetness of his armpit right through her t-shirt, and her stomach wrenched.

"Now, don't worry about your friend. You just go back to your home in America and leave me to take care of him for you," he said.

She couldn't bring herself to thank him but nodded her head. She had accomplished what she could for Jeevan. Smiling briefly at the woman with the fan, she left the office.

She glanced at the courthouse clock. Two-forty-five. Not enough time for another call if she were to make the bus. A feeling of loss, like an incredible hollowness, came over her, silent and cold. The noises of the street reached her through ears stuffed with cotton, and she felt as if a glass wall surrounded her, cutting her off from everyone and everything. The fear that had now become so normal, so comforting, really, in its familiarity, began to rise again from the hollow, silent spot inside her. It swelled, sucking her energy to feed itself, bulging inside her until she thought she would burst wide open, every part of her strewn on the dirt road at her feet. She longed for the feel of arms around her, pulling the pieces back together, making her whole again.

"Jamaica 'ave a lesson to teach yuh." It was as if all that had happened in Jamaica had been designed to wrench all her supports from beneath her, leaving her totally alone to face her fears. But wasn't that the lesson she had come here to learn? That she could face her fears and still go on? She could get to Montego. She could get on that plane, and she could get herself home. Alone. The bus rattled up to the curb in front of her. She walked toward its open door, and grabbing onto the railing, she took a step forward and began her long journey back.

EPILOGUE

Joanna heaved the last grocery bag onto the table, slipped out of her jacket, and hung it on the peg at the top of the stairs. She leaned down to look out a hallway window at the park below. The leaves had only now begun to fall, but the days were already growing shorter. She walked the few steps to the end of the hall, pulling down shades against the coming dark.

In the kitchen, she opened the refrigerator and shoved the milk behind the butter. The empty spaces inside seemed to taunt her now that Michael had moved out. She closed the fridge and stared at the photos stuck to the door. In one, Reggae romped as a puppy; in another, Jeevan, Dahlia, and the baby seemed the perfect family. She wondered if the lawyer had ever gotten Jeevan out of jail. She ran her finger over the photo of her and Michael smiling in the Jamaican sun. A Carol King song drifted through her mind, "It's too late, baby, now it's too late." She rubbed a tear away and sang softly, "Though we really did try to make it." She sighed. It had actually been over a long time ago. She had just been too afraid to see it. When she got back, they tried counseling one more time. But it had become painfully clear that although they loved each other, they wanted very different things. Her fear had blinded Joanna for too long to the truth.

She turned at a noise at the door downstairs. Probably the mailman. She hesitated at the top step, flipped the switch, and shivered in the dim light despite the warmth of the stairwell. Outside, she opened the mailbox, and slipped her hand in. Yelping, she jumped back and stuck her finger in her mouth, sucking on the tip. She shook it, and a tiny drop of blood seeped out.

"Damn!"

The low slant of the autumn sun cast a shadow over the mailbox. She peered in but saw nothing but envelopes. She leafed through a stack of bills. But, midway through the batch, she flinched. The envelopes fluttered to the ground. Eyeing the pile, she nudged it with her foot. She leaned over to gather the letters, staring at the one with a Jamaican postmark. She hurried back inside, slammed the door closed, and sank onto the bottom step. The fading sunlight flickered through the transom above the door, splashing hazy waves against the walls of the stairwell. She turned the envelope over to see the return address: *Frome, Westmoreland, Jamaica.*

Her fingers shook as she ripped open the flap. A chill seemed to rise from the paper itself, and she rubbed her hand against her knee. She turned the letter over to look at the signature. Dahlia! It was a three-page harangue, but one section in particular made Joanna pale: "Jeevan beat me and fight me off for a girl in the hills. But still I hope all the disadvantages you get me will pay back to you too."

Joanna let the letter dangle from her hand. She sat very still, staring at the blank wall in front of her. A silhouette flitted against the white background, beating wings in a mad panic. Joanna jerked around. A moth darted frantically around the bare light bulb. A moth? Her heart pounded and bitter bile rose in her throat. She jumped up. No. She wasn't doing this anymore. She pushed her hair back from her face and took a deep breath.

"Well, Dahlia, you got your wish, but somehow it turned out to be what I needed." She slipped the letter back in the envelope and went upstairs to finish unpacking the groceries.

ABOUT THE AUTHOR

Judy Goodrobb has been managing editor of a policy journal for 24 years and previously worked in public relations for several universities and non-profits. She has tutored writing at Pennsylvania State University, Philadelphia Community College, and Johnson State College in Vermont. She holds a B.A. in English literature from Temple University and an M.A. in writing from Vermont College of Norwich University. When she's not writing, she likes to play in the dirt raising vegetables and flowers in her garden.

Made in the USA
Columbia, SC
01 June 2023